Toby
Takes the Cake

"Toby, keep an eye on this sourdough bread. It will be ready in forty-five minutes."

"Gotcha!" Toby said as she practiced a demi-plié.

"The timer is set," her mother reminded her. "Just take out the bread when it rings."

"Right-o!" Toby saluted her mother. When her parents left, Toby gazed dreamily out the window, watching the first spring bluebird fly by.

"I wonder if my angel will be a bird like Rachel's," Toby said out loud. She turned on the radio and found a station playing a lovely passage from the ballet *Swan Lake*.

She turned up the music and danced four pirouettes, one after another. As Toby spun around, she remembered to focus her eyes on one spot and always return to that spot to keep from getting dizzy.

People who passed by and looked in the window saw a long-legged, long-haired girl dancing wildly. Toby totally lost track of time.

When her parents came back an hour later, Toby was still dancing around. "Hi, Mom! Hi, Dad!" she called out.

Mr. Antonio sniffed the air. "I smell something burning."

"Uh-oh!" Toby stopped midpirouette and raced to the oven. When she opened the door, smoke poured out.

ANGEL CORNERS

Toby Takes the Cake

BY FRAN MANUSHKIN

PUFFIN BOOKS

PUFFIN BOOKS
Published by the Penguin Group
Penguin Books USA Inc., 375 Hudson Street, New York, New York 10014, U.S.A.
Penguin Books Ltd, 27 Wrights Lane, London W8 5TZ, England
Penguin Books Australia Ltd, Ringwood, Victoria, Australia
Penguin Books Canada Ltd, 10 Alcorn Avenue, Toronto, Ontario, Canada M4V 3B2
Penguin Books (N.Z.) Ltd, 182-190 Wairau Road, Auckland 10, New Zealand

Penguin Books Ltd, Registered Offices: Harmondsworth, Middlesex, England

First published in the United States of America by Puffin Books,
a division of Penguin Books USA Inc., 1995
Published by arrangement with Chardiet Unlimited, Inc.

1   3   5   7   9   10   8   6   4   2

LIBRARY OF CONGRESS CATALOGING-IN-PUBLICATION DATA
Manushkin, Fran.
Toby takes the cake / by Fran Manushkin.
p.   cm. — (Angel Corners)
Summary: When she is afraid that she will lose the starring role in a ballet
recital and her family's bakery begins to lose business, Toby turns to her
friends in the Angel Club and to her very own guardian angel.
ISBN 0-14-037199-0
[1. Guardian angels—Fiction.   2. Angels—Fiction.   3. Friendship—Fiction.]
I. Title.   II. Series: Manushkin, Fran.   Angel Corners.
PZ7.M3195To   1995   [Fic]—dc20   94-38212   CIP   AC

Set in the United States of America

For Ellen Levine, definitely an angel!

CONTENTS

1

Toby Antonio, Ballerina?

Springtime in Angel Corners is prettier than springtime anywhere else on earth!

All along Main Street, daffodils trumpet the season with their yellow horns, and purple lilacs scent the air with their sweet perfume.

And the famous waterfall, Angel Falls, is bubblier than ever. It shimmers all the way down Hickory Hill.

But no sight *this* spring was happier than Toby Antonio's face when Madame Maximova announced to her ballet class: "As you know, I have taught all of you the steps for the lead role in *The Firebird*. I am now going to announce the name of the girl who will play the part at our spring recital."

Madame Maximova paused for drama.

"The lead will be"—she paused again—"Toby Antonio!"

Toby blushed—and beamed! For one of the rare moments in her life, she was speechless.

"Way to go!" Sasha Kirstein said, and patted Toby on the back. "You deserve it. Everyone knows you're the best dancer in class!"

"Really?" Felicia McWithers scowled, but no one paid any attention to her.

"Toby, I expect you to work hard," Madame Maximova said.

"Don't worry, I *will*," Toby promised, her green eyes flashing. Her freckled face was shiny with excitement. "I'll think about dancing twenty-four hours a day."

And Toby kept her word.

That day she didn't walk home from class. She danced! Her long dark braid flew behind her as she performed little leaps along Angel Stream. Toby knew she was showing off, but she enjoyed it.

When Toby reached Main Street, she pirouetted around Derek Weatherby's newsstand.

"Bravo!" he said, and applauded.

"Thank you!" Toby curtsied gracefully. "Derek, will you come to my dance recital?"

"You've got it! With bells on!" Derek promised.

As soon as he said the word *bells,* the angel clock

on top of Town Hall began chiming, *Bing! Bing! Bing! Bing!*

Toby and Derek watched together as a little blue door opened, and four gilded angels came out. They twirled in a graceful circle and then glided back inside.

Toby smiled up at the clock. It was working again, thanks to the members of the Angel Club. Toby and her friends Rachel Summers, Valentine McCall, and Lulu Bliss had helped raise the money to fix it.

Wait until I tell Rachel I got the lead! Toby said to herself. She said good-bye to Derek and hurried up Hickory Hill to Rachel's house to spread the news.

Rachel had only recently moved to Angel Corners, but she was already Toby's best friend. Rachel was one of the smallest girls in fifth grade and Toby was the tallest. But they made a great duo. They loved all the same things: sports, animals, and books. And underneath Rachel's shy exterior, she was very feisty, which Toby admired.

Rachel, wearing jeans and a Los Angeles Lakers T-shirt, was out in her front yard with a big white dog. Though Rachel was holding the leash, the dog seemed to be walking *her!*

"Hey, Rachel!" Toby shouted. "Guess what? I'm a star! I mean, I'm going to star in our ballet recital!"

"That is so great!" Rachel ran toward Toby with a big grin.

The dog got into the spirit by leaping up and licking Toby's face. "Hercules, down!" Toby commanded. "You've gotten so big!"

Rachel yanked on the Siberian husky's leash. "Mayor Witty sent Hercules to Mom for some obedience training!" Rachel's mom was the Angel Corners veterinarian, and Rachel helped her out quite a lot.

"Isn't it amazing?" said Toby. "Just a few months ago, Hercules was such a sick puppy, we didn't think he would live."

"Right." Rachel gave Hercules a pat. "But then Merrie came and saved him. She saved me, too!"

Merrie was Rachel's guardian angel. When Rachel moved to Angel Corners, she'd had a terrible time adjusting. It was hard being the new girl in school. And on top of that, Rachel's dad had recently died in a traffic accident. Merrie had been sent down from the Angel Academy in Heaven to help her.

Toby remembered that when Rachel had first told her about Merrie, she didn't believe her. But then, one day, near Angel Falls, the whole Angel Club got a glimpse of Merrie. She was spectacular!

Rachel waved her hand in front of Toby's eyes. "Earth to Toby!"

Toby Takes the Cake

"I'm here," she answered quickly. "I was just thinking about Merrie."

"Can I come to your dance recital?" Rachel asked.

"Of course! I'll save seats for you and the whole Angel Club—and for Merrie, too."

"Merrie doesn't need a chair!" Rachel reminded Toby. "She's fine floating in the air."

"Right!" Toby began dancing away. "Listen, I've got to go! Mom and Dad want me back at the bakery by five."

"See you tomorrow," Rachel said. "Come on, Hercules. It's time for more training!"

As Rachel tugged at the dog's leash, Toby rushed away to her family's bakery. It was just a few blocks down, next door to her house.

"Guess what?" Toby shouted, banging the screen door.

"What?" Mr. Antonio glanced up from a chocolate cake he was decorating.

"Did we win the lottery?" asked Mrs. Antonio hopefully.

"Something better," Toby answered. "Madame Maximova chose me to play the lead role in *The Firebird!*"

"Bravo!" Her dad waved his pastry tube around.

"Good going!" Toby's mom broke into a smile. "We can use some good news around here."

"What do you mean?" Toby asked. She didn't like the tone in her mother's voice.

"Oh, Mrs. Lewis just called and canceled her pastry order for her gardening club. She's going to serve fresh fruit instead because it's healthier. It seems that whenever the phone rings, someone else is canceling an order."

"That's awful!" Toby grabbed a white apron and tied it on over her leotard and tights. She had been helping out in her family's bakery since she was small.

Everybody in Angel Corners agreed that Mr. and Mrs. Antonio baked the best breads and pastries in town. And they were always very friendly and generous. Whenever a child craved a chocolate chip cookie but couldn't pay for it, Mrs. Antonio would say, "Bring the money tomorrow," or the next week, or whenever.

And if somebody lost a job, Mr. Antonio made sure that person's family still had bread on the table. "Pay when you can," he would tell them.

But that day, as Toby's mom was going over their accounts, she was bemoaning their generosity. "Money pours *out* of here like sugar," she sighed, "but it trickles *in* slower than molasses."

Toby wasn't really listening, though. Her thoughts were still on ballet. "I promised Madame Maximova I would practice every minute I could, and I will!" she declared.

Toby Takes the Cake

As she took each tray of dinner rolls out of the oven, Toby did a deep plié (a move Toby once described to Rachel as a fancy knee bend).

She loved the powerful feeling of her leg muscles. As always, or almost always, Toby remembered to keep her back perfectly straight.

At the sight of her cat, Michael Jordan, sitting outside on the window box, however, Toby's mind suddenly leaped to basketball. She'd named him after her favorite basketball player. As Toby plucked each dinner roll off the tray, she pretended to slam-dunk it into the bread basket.

"Toby!" warned her mother, "stop playing with the merchandise. Those rolls are the family's bread and butter."

"Bread and butter! That's a joke." Toby laughed. "Get it?"

"It's no joke, Toby." Her father's face was grim. "We can't afford to waste a penny."

"Sorry," Toby said, seeing her parents so serious.

Just then, Ms. McWithers, Felicia's mother, came into the bakery. She had straight blonde hair like Felicia's, and a similar snooty attitude.

"Are my cookies ready yet?" she asked in a loud brassy voice.

"No." Mr. Antonio glanced at the clock. "It's just after four o'clock. You ordered them for six. I haven't even put them in the oven."

"Well, I want them now!" Ms. McWithers insisted. "If you can't give them to me right away, I'm canceling my order." Ms. McWithers turned on her heels to go. "I'll buy my cookies at Downey's Bakery instead."

Then Ms. McWithers glared at Toby. "It's such a shame Felicia didn't get the lead role in the ballet! I bought her such a beautiful costume, too!"

Ms. McWithers huffed out, slamming the door behind her. Toby rolled her eyes, and her dad shook his head. "Felicia's furious that I got the lead in *The Firebird,*" Toby explained. "She wanted it so badly, but since Felicia never practices, how could she expect to get picked?"

Toby's mom took off her apron. "Come on," she told Mr. Antonio. "We're going to be late for our eye exams. Dr. Watson let us have his last appointment of the day, so Toby could be here to watch the bakery."

Toby's dad slipped a tray into the oven. "Toby, keep an eye on this sourdough bread. It will be ready in forty-five minutes."

"Gotcha!" Toby said as she practiced a demi-plié, which is half a plié.

"The timer is set," her mother reminded her. "Just take out the bread when it rings."

"Right-o!" Toby saluted her mother. When her parents left, Toby gazed dreamily out the window, watching the first spring bluebird fly by. It reminded her of Merrie, Rachel's angel, who had first appeared as a tiny red bird.

"I wonder if my angel will be a bird," Toby said out loud. She turned on the radio and found the classical music station. It was playing a lovely passage from the ballet *Swan Lake*. *A swan would be great!* Toby thought.

She turned up the music and danced four pirouettes, one after the other. She was pretending to be Odile, the glamorous black swan in the ballet.

As Toby spun around, she remembered to "spot." She kept her eyes on one spot, and always returned her focus to it while spinning. That kept her from getting dizzy.

People who passed by the bakery and looked in the window saw a long-legged, long-haired, freckle-faced girl dancing wildly. Toby totally lost track of time.

When her parents came back, an hour later, Toby was still dancing around. "Hi, Mom! Hi, Dad!" she called out.

Mr. Antonio sniffed the air. "I smell something burning."

"Uh-oh!" Toby stopped midpirouette and raced to the oven. When she opened the door, smoke poured out.

"You burned the sourdough bread!" shouted her

mother. "I *told* you to take it out when the timer went off."

"Oh, gosh!" Toby moaned. "I had the radio on so loud I didn't hear it."

Her dad dumped the bread into the garbage can. "That was a special order for Henricci's Restaurant. What am I going to tell them? 'Sorry, I can't send over your order. My daughter was dancing and let your bread burn'?"

Toby had never seen her father so angry.

"Toby, your mother and I warned you about fooling around. You are grounded for the next two weeks!"

"Dad, I'm sorry!" Toby apologized. "I'll be careful from now on."

"It's too late for that," said her mother angrily. "We've explained over and over that we can't afford to waste a penny."

"I'm really sorry!" Toby felt awful about being so careless. And she felt horrible about being punished.

She unlaced her apron and went running up to her room, where she could be alone.

The happiest day in her life had suddenly become totally awful!

CHAPTER

2

Curtains!

The next day, things got even worse. When Toby came down to breakfast, she saw her dad grumbling to himself. He was sitting at his desk, paying bills.

"I have some bad news," he told Toby. "I've just written a check for this semester's ballet lessons. Madame Maximova was nice enough to let us pay her late. But she wrote a note saying she can't do it again next semester. She has bills to pay, too."

"So, what does that mean?" Toby asked nervously.

Her father sighed. "It means that we can't send you to ballet class next semester, Toby. Your mother and I simply don't have the money."

"But Dad," Toby said frantically, "I've taken ballet for as long as I can remember!"

"I know." Mr. Antonio's face looked pained. "But we have no choice. We have to cut back our spending. All our money has to go to buy bakery supplies. Otherwise, we can't stay in business. If things pick up, maybe you can go back next year. Toby, I'm really sorry."

Toby swallowed back a sob, then rushed off to school in a state of shock. Nothing so horrible had ever happened to her in her life!

She got to class just as the bell rang. Rachel, Lulu, and Val could tell something was wrong. Toby's green eyes had lost their sparkle. And her feet, which usually danced restlessly beneath her desk, were totally still.

What's wrong? Rachel wrote in a note.

Toby wrote back:

Catastrophe! I'll tell you at lunch.

When the lunch bell rang, the Angel Club rushed to the cafeteria together.

"What happened?" Rachel asked anxiously.

Toby took a deep breath. First, she told them about burning the bread and being grounded. Then she explained how badly the bakery was doing and that her ballet lessons were coming to an end.

"That's awful!" Rachel cried. "I can't imagine you not dancing."

Toby's eyes filled with tears. "Neither can I!"

Rachel rummaged in her backpack and took out a rumpled tissue. "Here," she offered, handing it to her friend.

As Toby dabbed at her eyes, Lulu and Val patted her on the back.

Suddenly Rachel made a decision. "Let's have an emergency meeting of the Angel Club this afternoon."

"Why?" sniffled Toby.

"So we can find a way to help you."

"But what can the Angel Club do?" asked Val.

"A lot!" Rachel's eyes flashed with determination. "We made money to help fix the angel clock, didn't we? That was our very first project. Well, our second project can be Toby!"

"That's a great idea!" Lulu chimed in, running her hand through her persistently rumpled hair.

Toby perked up a little. "You are all such good friends!"

"Let's meet at my house right after school," Rachel suggested. "Can everyone come?"

"Yes!" Val and Lulu said together.

"But we have to make it a fast meeting," Toby reminded them, "since I'm grounded."

"No problem," everyone agreed.

Just then Andrea Nesbit, a small pale girl with mousy brown hair, came over to sit with them. She wore a faded blue jumper and holey sneakers.

"Hi, Andrea!" Toby said, and smiled at her.

Andrea smiled back shyly.

"How is your dad doing?" Rachel asked.

"He's feeling a lot better," Andrea answered. Just a few months ago, Andrea had been almost a slave to Felicia McWithers because Felicia threatened to tell everyone that Andrea's father was in a hospital because of emotional problems. "He's home now, but he's still out of work."

"My folks are worried about being out of work, too," said Toby. "But at least your dad's home, Andrea. That's good news."

Everyone concentrated on eating lunch. Toby didn't have much of an appetite. After nibbling her sandwich, she unwrapped a huge brownie. When she noticed Andrea eyeing it, Toby said, "Here, Andrea, would you like this?"

"Thanks!" said Andrea. "Do you mind if I take it with me? I'm supposed to meet somebody on the playground."

"Go ahead," Toby said. As Andrea hurried away, Rachel leaned forward and whispered to Toby, "Andrea has a new friend."

"I noticed." Toby nodded. "It's Sylvie Sawyer.

I've seen them together after school and in the library."

"Sylvie's hair is so cool," Lulu said. Sylvie wore her hair in tight, neat cornrows that perfectly out-lined the shape of her head. "I'm so glad Andrea got out of Felicia's clutches."

"I second that," Rachel said. Rachel had shown Andrea that she didn't *have* to be afraid of people knowing the truth about her father. That had made Felicia furious. Of course, lots of things made Felicia furious.

In fact, at this very moment Felicia was sitting by herself, glaring at Toby and Rachel. She was jingling her many silver bracelets as she combed her blonde ponytail.

Soon the bell rang, and everyone hurried back to class.

When school was over, the Angel Club walked to Rachel's house together.

"Let's have our meeting in the kitchen," Rachel suggested. Her mom's veterinary office was in the back of the house, with its own entrance. Still, the walls were thin, and animal sounds traveled to the kitchen.

"The squawks you hear are coming from Derek Weatherby's cockatoo," Rachel explained. "Just try to ignore him."

"As if we could!" Lulu rolled her eyes.

"Okay," Rachel said. "Does everyone have enough apple juice and cookies? Good. Since the meeting's at my house, I'll call it to order. Does anyone have any ideas on how we can help Toby with her ballet lessons?"

Lulu's hand shot up. "I have one! Let's make a funny home video and send it to that TV show *America's Silliest Videos.* If we win a big prize, we can give the money to Toby."

"But what if we don't win?" said practical Val. "It would be fun to try, but I think we need something closer to home."

"I guess you're right," Lulu admitted. Her dad owned Starlight Video, and Lulu was a total movie and TV freak. She was determined to be a director when she grew up.

Rachel jumped up. "I have an idea! Back in Los Angeles our school had a car wash to raise money for a girl who needed a brain operation. Without the operation, she would have died! Maybe we can have a car wash for you, Toby."

Toby said, "Rachel, you're terrific to think of that, but my ballet lessons aren't exactly a matter of life or death."

"Yes, they are!" Rachel said loyally. "I mean, they are *to you!*"

Val thoughtfully licked a cookie crumb from the corner of her mouth, then said, "Maybe I can write about you in my stepfather's newspaper. I'm starting my own column soon. It's called 'The Fifth Grade Insider'."

"Please don't!" Toby said quickly. "Mom and Dad would be so embarrassed, and so would I!"

"But we have to do something!" Val insisted.

"Can anyone think of any other ideas?" Rachel asked.

Nobody could.

"I've got to get home," said Toby, "seeing as how I'm grounded."

Rachel was disappointed. "Well, then, I guess we should all go home and think about it some more."

"Toby, we won't let you down!" Val promised. "When the Angel Club is on a case, we never give up!"

As Rachel walked Toby to the door, she said wistfully, "Wouldn't this be a great time for your guardian angel to come?"

"Definitely!" Toby responded.

"Look for a little red bird," Rachel suggested. "Remember, that's how *my* guardian angel came!"

"I know. I'll keep watching," Toby promised. When Toby opened the front door to her house, she was practically knocked down by her older brother, Brian, who was rushing out.

"Hey, watch it!" Toby yelled.

"Sorry," Brian blurted. "I've got to get out of

here! There's a red bird in the backyard making an incredible racket. I'm having trouble enough doing my homework without that."

"Did you say a red bird?" Toby's eyes lit up.

"Yeah! A redheaded woodpecker."

"Brian, thanks! Thanks a lot." Toby raced around to the back.

Brian shrugged. "I always knew you had a screw loose," he said.

That bird has to be my guardian angel! Toby thought. She found the woodpecker right away, hammering on the trunk of an old crab apple tree. It would have been hard to miss, with its bright head.

"Hi!" Toby waved. The bird ignored her and hopped farther up the tree. "Are you my guardian angel? Please say yes! I need you so much! If I have to give up ballet, I don't know what I'll do. Can't you help me? Please?"

Queeeeeek! the woodpecker squawked, and flew away.

"Come back!" Toby shouted, and she leaped away after the bird. "See how high I can jump? I was born to be a dancer. You've just *got* to help me!" Toby pleaded.

But the bird flew on, ignoring her. Toby chased the woodpecker halfway up Hickory Hill. She watched it pause for a quick drink from the stream and then fly away over Angel Falls.

Toby Takes the Cake

"Darn!" Toby felt so disappointed. She sat down near the stream and watched the waterfall. Her eyes filled with tears, threatening to become mini-waterfalls themselves. "I need my angel so much." Toby sighed. "Where *is* she?"

3

Soul Mates Class

"**Y**our angel is coming very soon!" declared Florinda, the Queen of the Angels. In fact, at that moment, she was flying to the Crystal Classroom to meet with her angels-in-training.

Florinda's silver dress and beautiful brown face gleamed in the rays of the setting sun as she flew through the halls of the Angel Academy. She flew directly into the Crystal Classroom, landing gracefully at her silver desk. *This is the perfect time to pick Toby's angel,* Florinda thought. "Advanced Soul Mates class is about to begin," she announced in her powerful voice.

Merrie, Rachel's guardian angel, came flying into the room first. As usual, her turquoise gown was rumpled and her long red hair needed a complete combing.

"I came to give you a progress report on Rachel Summers!" Merrie sang excitedly in her high, light voice. "Rachel has so many friends now, and with my help, she's singing a lot louder so everyone can hear her lovely voice. In fact, she may sing a solo in the school concert next semester. And Rachel isn't afraid of the woods anymore, thanks to me. And I have so much more to tell you—"

"I'm sure you do," Florinda interrupted gently. "But class is about to start. You can tell us more about it later." Merrie had been the first angel-in-training to visit Angel Corners. Florinda didn't want to stifle Merrie's enthusiasm, but she had to focus on Toby right now.

As soon as Serena, Celeste, and Amber flew to their seats, Florinda told them all to gaze down at Toby, through the clear crystal floor of the class-room. "Today, our Soul Mates class is going to be devoted to choosing Toby's guardian angel. Kindly raise your hand if you think you qualify for the job."

"I do! I do!" Celeste's hand shot up into the air. Celeste had thick black hair and wore a very ruffly green gown. "I've been watching Toby, and I know I'd be perfect for her."

"Really? Why?" Florinda asked.

"Because I love to dance! Just like Toby! And I

think her family is such fun! I love them!"

"Especially Toby's brothers," added Merrie. "Celeste is boy-crazy."

"I am not!" Celeste proclaimed, but she blushed a bright pink.

Amber raised her hand and said in her calm, deliberate voice, "I think I would be Toby's perfect soul mate. I love animals. Michael Jordan and I would get along perfectly! And I'm always well organized and I study hard . . . but we all do that. Gosh, maybe those aren't good enough reasons."

Florinda nodded. "That's correct, Amber. Those aren't sufficient reasons, and it was wise of you to see that."

Amber nodded and smoothed down her silky amber dress, which perfectly matched her amber hair and amber eyes. Sometimes Amber was a little *too* well organized!

"Serena," said Florinda gently. "You have been very quiet. The last time I chose a guardian angel, you were quite eager to go."

"I know," Serena answered softly, gazing down at her lap. Her ivory gown was immaculate, as usual. "I guess I don't think I'm right for this assignment."

"I know why you say that," Celeste burst out. "Toby is so athletic and rough-and-tumble. And you wouldn't want to get near a working bakery.

You're afraid you'd mess up your dress."

"That's not true!" Serena glared, her emerald green eyes furious.

"Then what's wrong?" asked Florinda kindly.

Serena shrugged, her pretty, rosy face gazing at her lap again. "I was hoping to be Val's guardian angel. Val is so careful about the way she looks. I just love her lacy canopy bed! And all the clothes her mother brings her from exotic places."

"See? All you care about is appearances," Celeste said spitefully, fluffing out her ruffles and straightening her own ribbons.

"Serena, look at me," said Florinda tenderly.

Serena gazed up into Florinda's calm face.

"Now," said Florinda, "tell me how you feel about Toby, not her clothes or her house or her cat, but *her.*"

Serena answered thoughtfully, "I *like* Toby. She is smart and cheerful. And when Rachel needed a friend, Toby was there. And of course, she's a wonderful dancer."

Florinda replied, "That is all true. But more important than that, Serena, you should see the way your eyes light up when you speak about Toby. I think you are the perfect guardian angel for her."

"I am?" Serena liked to be praised, because even angels can feel insecure at times.

"Yes," Florinda continued, "I think you and Toby are soul mates. When you visit earth, you will notice many friends and couples who seem totally mismatched. But if you study them for a while, you will see why they work."

"Can I go right away?" Serena was beginning to get excited.

"Of course, Toby needs you! But first, I'd like us to review the Angel Rules."

"I know them all by heart," Serena insisted.

"Well, just in case . . ." said Florinda, pointing to the silver chalkboard.

"Rule number one: go slowly! Humans need time to get used to their guardian angels. We are always so surprising to them.

"Rule number two: you can take any form that you want. Serena, you can be a crocodile, or a cloud, or you can be yourself.

"Rule number three: you cannot be seen or heard by anyone except the child to whom you are assigned. As you know, I bent that rule slightly for Merrie so the whole Angel Club could see her. But I won't do it again."

Merrie glowed as the pleasure of feeling special washed over her.

Celeste sulked. "It seems like I'm never going to earth. Never, never, never!"

Florinda spoke to her kindly. "You and Toby are

just too much alike, dear. Both of you are so dramatic. If I sent you to her, the result would be total chaos and confusion!"

"I *like* confusion!" Celeste kicked at her ruffles.

Amber patted down her dress. "I guess I can wait a little longer. It's only been a hundred years, eleven months, four days, six hours, and twenty minutes."

Merrie rushed over to hug Serena good-bye. "You are going to have such fun! You can fall out of trees, sing inside teakettles—"

"I'll do no such thing!" Serena said, glaring. "I intend to be a dignified guardian angel."

"Well, la-di-da!" Merrie rolled her eyes.

Florinda drew Serena close, enveloping her in her motherly wings. "Good luck," she whispered. "And I hope you *will* have some fun. Being an angel isn't all work, you know!"

"Bon voyage! Happy landings!" Merrie and the other angels chimed in.

Then Serena floated out of the Crystal Classroom and flew serenely down to earth.

CHAPTER

4

One Angel, Coming Up!

At that moment, Toby was walking away from Angel Falls and heading home. "I guess that bird wasn't my angel, after all," she said.

That night, Toby sat on her bed and looked at photos taken at her previous ballet recitals. The first one was taken when Toby was four. She had been a mouse in *The Nutcracker*. At five, Toby was a lot taller and wore a pink dress as a dancing rose. At age six she was a princess . . . Toby slammed the album shut. She couldn't bear to look anymore. How could she possibly give up ballet?

Toby stood up and tried a few steps from *The Firebird*. She had promised Madame Maximova to dance every spare minute, but she hadn't kept her promise. Michael Jordan danced along. "Oh, Mike," Toby said, flopping down in the chair again, "what am I going to do without ballet lessons?"

Her cat just stared at her. He didn't have an answer either.

The next morning before school started, the owner of the Angel Corners health club came into the bakery. "I can't order your blueberry muffins anymore," he told Mr. Antonio. "Nobody will eat them! They keep complaining about cholesterol. And I can't even give away Mrs. Antonio's apple turnovers. Nobody buys any."

Toby's dad groaned. "That's the third cancellation we've had this week!"

"Everyone is watching what they eat," said Toby's mom. "It's probably just a fad, but we are losing so much business."

Just then, Sally Jillian, the accountant, came in with a report of the bakery's finances. "Mr. Antonio, you have a big tax bill to pay next month. I hope things pick up soon."

"So do I!" Toby's dad looked really worried.

Toby had never seen her dad look so troubled. "Mom," she said nervously, "it's going to be okay, isn't it?"

"I hope so," Mrs. Antonio replied. "We won't lose the bakery or anything like that. . . ." But her voice sounded shaky. "I feel awful about you losing your lessons, Toby. Maybe next year—if things get better. Here"—she handed Toby a small box—"I made a little cake to cheer you up. It's your favorite: double chocolate fudge. Why don't you share it with your friends at lunch?"

"Mom, thanks!" Toby took the box and headed off to school. But the bakery's troubles stayed in her mind.

That day at school, Ms. Fisher announced, "Class, today we are starting a study of nutrition. I want each of you to choose a partner to research one aspect of the subject."

Val and Lulu waved to each other, their matching friendship bracelets dangling.

Andrea and Sylvie waved to each other, too. Today, they were wearing their hair almost the same way. Andrea had lots of thin braids now, too.

Toby paired up with Rachel, of course. Toby noticed that nobody wanted to be partners with Felicia.

"Now," continued Ms. Fisher, "can anyone name a mineral or vitamin or food you might study?"

"How about caviar?" Felicia suggested. "My mother always serves it at her parties. It costs a fortune!"

"Go ahead," said Ms. Fisher, aware that Felicia

was trying to impress the class. "And I want a *thorough* caviar report!"

"How about licorice twists?" yelled Sam Eisenstein.

"If you can find any nutritional value in them, go right ahead," Ms. Fisher said, playing along.

"I'd like to do cholesterol," Toby told Ms. Fisher. "Everyone is so worried about it."

"Good choice," observed Ms. Fisher.

At lunch that day, as they did almost every day, Toby, Rachel, Val, and Lulu hurried off to sit together.

Rachel asked, "Did anyone get any ideas about how to help Toby?"

Lulu shook her head, but Val said, "I have a glimmer of an idea. But first I want to do a little research in the library."

"What is it?" Lulu asked eagerly. "You can't keep secrets from me!"

"I'm not keeping it a secret," said Val. "In fact, I want you to come with me today." That calmed Lulu down right away. She took a giant bite of her hamburger.

"Whatever it is, I hope it works!" Toby said wistfully. "I've been so depressed, Mom tried to cheer me up by baking my favorite cake, a double chocolate fudge."

Toby carefully lifted the lid of the bakery box.

"Oh my!" she gasped. Pink frosting letters were forming on the cake right before her eyes. It was as if an invisible hand was writing them. Slowly, the letters spelled out:

One Angel
Coming Up!

"She's here!" Toby shouted.

"*Who's* here?" asked Rachel.

"My guardian angel!" Toby pointed. "She just wrote a message on my cake! In pink frosting!"

"Let me see!" Rachel said, jumping up. "Take the cake out of the box so we can see."

Toby reached in and lifted out the cake. And as she did, she saw the pink frosting letters grow dimmer, then disappear!

"Where's the writing?" asked Val, perplexed.

"I don't know!" Toby shook her head. "It disappeared when I took out the cake. How weird."

"It's not weird at all," said Rachel matter-of-factly. "Since this is *your* angel, only you can see her writing."

"Oh, Rachel!" Lulu blurted. "You think you know everything, just because your angel already came."

"I'm sorry!" Rachel flushed pink. "I was only trying to help."

"Don't worry!" said sensible Val. "Remember

how complicated everything was with Merrie? I'm sure Toby's angel will be back! In the meantime, I'd love a piece of that cake, Toby. Maybe it will bring us all luck."

"I bet it will! Let's invite Andrea and Sylvie to have some, too." Toby rushed over to where they were sitting. "Come on over and have some cake," Toby suggested.

"Thanks!" they both said eagerly, and got up to join the Angel Club.

"I like your matching cornrows," Val told them.

"Sylvie braided them for me," Andrea said, as Sylvie's pretty brown face shone proudly.

Later, as they went back to class, Rachel asked Toby, "I wonder what your angel looks like? Do you think she'll have red hair, like Merrie?"

"I don't care what color hair she has!" Toby declared. "I just want her to come!"

All afternoon in class, Toby kept her eye on the blackboard, hoping her angel would write another message. But the only words she saw were in Ms. Fisher's slanty handwriting.

When it was time for a spelling test, Toby hoped a special message would appear on her paper—such as the right answers!

But it didn't.

During study time, Toby and Rachel researched cholesterol in the library. Toby read aloud to

Rachel: "Cholesterol is a fatty substance produced by the human body that is also contained in foods. High cholesterol is a major risk factor in heart disease. A common source of cholesterol is egg yolks. The saturated fats in milk and cream can contribute to high cholesterol levels in the human body."

"Hmm," Toby said, "so that's why people are worried." Toby couldn't imagine how her parents were going to solve this problem. The bakery used eggs, milk, and cream in almost everything.

After school, Toby and Rachel walked home together. As they headed down Main Street, sharing an ice-cream bar, Andrea passed by, all alone. She looked as if she'd been crying.

"What's wrong?" Toby asked her.

"Uh . . . hi . . ." Andrea looked down at her holey sneakers. "Um . . . my friend . . . uh . . . Sylvie and I . . . we had a kind of fight."

Felicia, who was coming out of the candy shop, smirked. "Andrea, I *told* you nobody else would be your friend. Not when they found out about your weird family."

Felicia began walking away, then she suddenly stopped and turned around. "It's a pity you're not my friend anymore, Andrea. I happen to have front-row tickets for the circus *and* a rock concert. And I *was* looking for someone to take along."

Toby Takes the Cake

Andrea looked longingly after Felicia.

"Don't go!" Rachel blurted out. She put her arm around Andrea's narrow shoulders. "It may sound like fun, but you know Felicia."

"Right!" Toby added. "We certainly know Felicia!"

"You'll be sorry you said that, Toby Antonio!" Felicia glared and stomped away.

Andrea cleared her throat nervously. "My dad is still looking for a job, and we never have money for treats. It would be so nice to go somewhere special."

"I know," Toby said sympathetically. "What did you and Sylvie fight about?"

"I . . . I can't tell you!" Tears began streaming down Andrea's face, and she turned and ran away.

"I wish we could help her," said Rachel longingly. "I know how it feels to lose a friend. Remember our big fights, Toby?"

"How could I forget?" Toby rolled her eyes. "They were horrible."

"Maybe the Angel Club can help Andrea. Should we talk about it at our next meeting?"

"Sure," Toby agreed. "But right now you and I are going to play basketball. I want to teach you some new moves."

When they reached Toby's house, they began shooting baskets at the hoop on the Antonios' garage.

"I'm going to teach you how to dribble with either hand," Toby said. "That way, you can use your size against the taller players, by weaving in and out and all around them."

"Really? Being small can be an advantage? I love that idea!" Rachel said enthusiastically.

Rachel and Toby worked hard for an hour or so, with Michael Jordan leaping around them. He was not playing basketball, though. He was chasing flies.

"I need a rest!" Rachel gasped. Her blonde bangs were plastered against her forehead. Toby was flushed and tired, too.

As they drank from their water bottles, Rachel said to Toby, "I wonder what Lulu and Val are up to. Val said she had an idea about how to help you."

"Who knows? But when they get to working together," Toby said, "stand back! They usually come up with something amazing."

Plotting in the Library

At that very moment, Val and Lulu were hurrying to the Angel Corners library.

"Val! When are you going to tell me your secret plan?" Lulu asked eagerly.

"Soon!" Val assured her. "I didn't want to tell you before because you might have blabbed it around."

"*Moi?*" Lulu asked, imitating Miss Piggy.

When they reached the library, Val rushed straight over to the reference section. Derek Weatherby was sitting there, reading from a huge book. "Hi!" Val and Lulu said, smiling. "What are you doing?"

"I'm doing some important research," Derek

told them. Derek owned, the newsstand on Main Street, but Angel Corners history was his hobby. He knew everything about the town.

"We came to do research, too," Val said eagerly.

Lulu groaned. "Val, if you don't tell me your plan right this minute, I'm going to scream!"

"Not in the library, please!" Derek teased, his face breaking into a grin.

"Okay! I'll tell you right now!" Val agreed. "Derek, maybe you can help us."

"I'll certainly try," he promised.

"Well, here goes," began Val. "Lulu and I want to help a friend of ours, who needs money for ballet class. Do you know where we can find a list of all the groups in town that give away money?"

"Like the Elks Club? Groups like that?" asked Derek.

"Right!" Val said.

"Easy as pie!" Derek got up and walked over to the shelf. He grabbed a green book and came right back. "Here you are!"

"You work fast!" Lulu said.

Derek shrugged. "I know my way around this library, that's for sure. I've been here every day reading up on how to start a new business. You see, I want to open up a bookstore."

"That would be terrific!" Val's eyes lit up. "We have to drive fifty miles to buy books."

36

"I'll be your first customer," Lulu promised. "As long as you stock lots of film books."

"You've got it!" Derek agreed.

"Now, let's get down to work," Val said. "My stepfather told me that lots of organizations in town give away money. So here's my plan: I want to find a group that offers money to ballet students."

Lulu punched her fist into the air. "You mean like a scholarship? Great idea, Val! You're a genius."

"I wouldn't go that far." Val opened the book and read the first name: "Angel Corners Moose Club: Contributes money to children's hospitals and marching bands."

"No good. Try the next one," said Lulu.

"Angel Corners Community Chest: Raises money for the Angel Corners library."

"Next!" Lulu urged.

Val went through all the town listings and then all the state listings. It took forty-five minutes, but she couldn't find one group that had anything to do with ballet.

"Well, it *was* a good idea!" Lulu said sadly.

"I haven't given up yet," Val insisted.

"That's what I like about you." Lulu perked up. "You're just like me—stubborn!"

"Are you girls having any luck?" Derek asked, glancing up from his book.

"No," Val said, "but we're not giving up!"

Lulu picked up the latest copy of the *Angel Corners Gazette*. "I love the wedding announcements!" she cooed. "They are so romantic! Hey, look." Lulu jabbed Val. "Here's the wedding announcement for Hortense Heft. Remember the summer she taught us how to ride horseback? Her family has buckets of money, but they're not snobby like Felicia and her mother."

"And they buy so many magazines!" Derek added. "Music and drama magazines, zillions of them."

"Hey, look!" Lulu said excitedly. "This wedding announcement says that Mrs. Heft raises money for the PTA and the Chamber of Commerce. Maybe she would give Toby some money."

"I'm afraid it's not that simple," Derek explained. "You see, Mrs. Heft gives money to groups and institutions, not to individuals."

"Oh!" Val's face fell.

"I'm sorry to be the bearer of bad news," Derek said. "I prefer good news at all times."

Lulu tried to console Val. "Maybe we can think of something else."

"I'll keep my eyes open, too," Derek promised. "I know how much those lessons mean to Toby."

Val looked at Lulu, and Lulu looked at Val. "How did you know it was Toby?" asked Val.

Derek winked. "Good luck," he said.

"Thanks," Val told him, as she and Lulu got up to go.

Slowly, the two of them walked home together, hoping to come up with something.

That night, after dinner, Rachel called Toby and asked, "Has your angel left any more messages?"

"No," Toby answered.

"Darn it. Maybe she'll come in a dream next, the way Merrie came to me."

"Maybe!" Toby said, trying to be hopeful. She decided to go to bed early to speed up the process. Toby braided her hair and put on a nightshirt right after her shower.

She waved good night to her poster of Michael Jordan and snuggled up with her own Michael. He purred like a little engine.

When Toby put out the light, she saw graceful silver shadows moving across her bedroom wall.

But the shadows didn't spell out any words. They were merely shadows of pine trees waving in the breeze outside the window.

Toby closed her eyes, humming the music to the ballet *Sleeping Beauty*.

And then she fell asleep.

CHAPTER

6

Felicia's No Angel

No angels appeared in Toby's dreams that night. And there was no angelic syrup-writing on Toby's breakfast pancakes. And no watercolor angel-writing on Toby's painting in art class.

She was very disappointed. And so were her friends in the Angel Club.

Up in the Angel Academy, the angels-in-training were simply perplexed.

"What's wrong with Serena?" Amber asked. "Why is she so slow?"

"I'm glad you asked that question," replied Florinda. She and her student angels were gathered around a huge well in the Wishing Pavilion. As they gazed down this well, they could see all of Angel Corners.

"As you know," Florinda began, "humans seem to wish for things all day long! It just goes with being human. Amber, can you tell me how people go about wishing on earth?"

"That's easy!" Amber said quickly. "They pull on wishbones! I see that all the time."

"Any other ways?" asked Florinda.

"They wish on stars," Merrie observed, "and they toss pennies into ponds and fountains."

"We know all that," said Celeste impatiently, "but what does it have to do with Serena and Toby?"

"I'll tell you in good time," Florinda scolded. "Now, the important fact is that we angels can grant some wishes right away, but not all of them. Fulfilling wishes is a very mysterious process."

Amber's eyes glowed. "I love mysteries!"

Florinda continued, "Now, we know Serena wants to appear to Toby, but she has to do it at just the right time! Serena likes to do everything very carefully."

"I know, I know," Celeste yawned.

"But I think something is about to happen," predicted Florinda. "Let's keep watching."

So they did.

The angels watched Toby hurry to ballet class to begin rehearsing her *Firebird* solos with Madame Maximova. Toby and Lulu walked out the school doors together. "Break a leg!" Lulu said, wishing her luck.

"Don't say that!" Toby groaned.

"I thought it meant good luck," said Lulu, perplexed. "I know it means good luck in the theater and in movies."

"Well, not in ballet!" Toby glared angrily.

"I'm sorry," Lulu apologized. "I always stick my foot in my mouth!"

Further along on her way to ballet class, Toby saw Sylvie and Andrea walking together. *They made up their fight,* Toby noticed. *That's great.*

When Toby reached the ballet studio, she rushed into the changing room to put on her blue leotard and pink tights. Felicia was already there, opening a box from Capezio. "A new outfit?" asked Toby with faked surprise.

Felicia didn't say anything at all, but made a face that was meant to shut Toby up. Toby suspected that Felicia took ballet only so she could wear frilly tutus. Once Felicia had come to class wearing diamond earrings. Madame Maximova had made her take them off. No jewelry was allowed in class.

Today Felicia was putting up her blonde ponytail with two glittery blue barrettes. Toby turned her back on Felicia and pinned her own braid up on top of her head. Madame Maximova needed to see the students' necks while they danced.

Toby put on pink leg warmers over her tights. When she entered the sunny ballet studio, she went straight to the barre and began stretching.

"Hi!" Sasha called over to Toby. "Are you excited about your solo? I'd be a nervous wreck if *I* were dancing the lead. I'd rather dance in a group, with the whole corps."

"I love performing." Toby grinned. "I'm a ham! Didn't you know that?"

Madame Maximova walked gracefully into the room. She was so slim and elegant in her soft gray dress and pulled-back silver-gray hair.

"Let us begin," she said in a formal voice, as she put on a tape for barre exercises.

Toby placed her feet in first position and the warm-ups began.

This was the moment in the week when Toby entered a different world. As she flexed and relaxed her muscles, she felt a sense of power. Her body responded so well. She felt so confident. That was one of the reasons Toby loved ballet so much.

Madame Maximova paced in front of the dancers, stopping now and then to correct someone's position. "Felicia," she said sternly, "I've told you over and over not to flop your arms around!

You're supposed to look like a rare and lovely bird—not like a barnyard chicken."

"I do *not* look like a chicken!" Felicia whined.

Sasha whispered to Toby, "Felicia is too busy admiring herself in the mirror to concentrate."

After warm-ups, Madame Maximova said, "I'm going to work with Toby alone for a while. The rest of you practice your roles in the corps de ballet."

"Begin," Madame Maximova told Toby, putting on the *Firebird* music, by Igor Stravinsky. The wild rhythms and quick tempos were so exciting to dance to!

Toby worked hard. Her freckled face was soon dripping with perspiration.

"Your arm movements are getting stronger," Madame said.

Toby flushed with pleasure. *All that basketball playing is great for my arm muscles,* she told herself.

"Now, class," announced Madame Maximova, "we will end today's session by practicing leaps."

All the dancers formed a line and one after another began jumping diagonally across the room.

Toby's legs were long, and they were strong, too, from running up and back on a basketball court. Toby could leap higher than anyone else in class.

"Students," said Madame Maximova, "I want you all to be seated for a moment and watch Toby.

She has such wonderful elevation. And notice how still her arms are. She doesn't wave them around."

Toby's jumps took her closer and closer to the line of girls sitting against the wall.

Suddenly something awful happened: She tripped over someone's foot and went flying!

"Ouch!" Toby shouted as she landed hard on her ankle and collapsed.

Madame Maximova rushed over to pick Toby up. As she did, she scolded, "Girls, how many times have I warned you *not* to stick your legs out into the middle of the floor?" She said to Toby, "See if you can put any weight on that leg."

"I can't!" Toby gasped in pain. "It really hurts!"

"Gee, I hope you didn't sprain your ankle," said Felicia in a sickly sweet voice.

"I'll put ice on it right away," said Madame Maximova. "That will keep down the swelling."

As Toby sat in Madame's office with an ice pack, her teacher gave her a worried look. "The recital isn't very far away. I hope your ankle is okay."

"It *has* to be!" Toby insisted.

Felicia rushed into the office and said, "I could dance the lead instead. I have the perfect costume. My mother bought it in New York."

Madame Maximova looked at her icily. "Don't be so eager to profit from someone else's accident, Felicia."

In the changing room, Sasha came over and told Toby that she had seen Felicia stick her foot out. "But it happened so fast I didn't have time to warn you."

"I'll *get* that creep if it's the last thing I do!" Toby promised.

"If I don't get her first," threatened Sasha.

Toby tested her injured foot. It felt awful, but she could get herself home if she put most of her weight on the other one.

As Toby limped past Rachel's house, she saw her friend out front exercising a Great Dane.

"What happened?" Rachel asked. "Whoa, Moose!" She tugged at the leash. "Why are you limping, Toby?"

"Felicia tripped me in ballet. I think I sprained my ankle."

Rachel's face flushed with anger. "Madame Maximova should throw her out of the class."

"She can't," said Toby, "because Felicia's dad is her landlord. He's threatened to triple Madame's rent if she kicks Felicia out of class."

"I'll help you walk home," Rachel offered. "Wait a sec, till I take Moose back to his cage."

When Rachel returned, she linked arms with Toby. "Lean on me," she encouraged her friend.

"It hurts so much." Toby's voice quivered. "And

the recital is only days away. I'm not sure my ankle will heal by then."

"It has to!" Rachel insisted fiercely. "I know how much this means to you." Rachel wanted so much to cheer Toby up, but how?

When they passed an empty lot, Rachel got an idea. She picked a bunch of dandelions, the kind with the fuzzy white seeds. "Here, Toby," she said optimistically. "Make a wish on these when you get home. Maybe it'll come true."

"Oh, Rachel," Toby answered grumpily, "blowing on dandelion seeds is just for little kids."

"Try it!" Rachel urged. "It can't hurt."

When they reached Toby's house, her mother asked, "What's wrong?"

"I hurt my ankle in ballet class," Toby told her. She didn't mention a word about Felicia. Toby hated to tattle.

"See you tomorrow." Rachel gave Toby a quick hug and left.

Toby's mom helped her daughter put more ice on her aching foot. Then Toby hobbled upstairs to the attic, where she could be alone. It was her own private ballet studio. Toby's grandmother had been a dancer, and she had built the studio many years ago. It had floor-to-ceiling mirrors, a ballet barre, a stereo, and a piano.

Toby collapsed onto a soft old armchair and closed her eyes. She felt so weary—and so worried! And now that she was all alone, all she could do was cry.

"How could Felicia be so mean?" she sobbed. "How could *anyone* be so mean?"

Toby cried until she had no tears left. When she opened her eyes again, the first thing she saw was the dandelion bouquet that Rachel had given her.

With her face still wet with tears, Toby picked up the bouquet, closed her eyes, and wished fiercely. "I want to see my guardian angel *right now!*"

Then she blew as hard as she could, making the feathery seeds fly toward the ceiling.

"Ah-choo!"

Toby heard a dainty sneeze. She opened her eyes and gazed up at the ceiling. There, floating serenely, was her guardian angel!

CHAPTER

7

Ah-Choo!

"*Ah-choo! Ah-choo!*" The angel sneezed in midair, holding a delicate lace handkerchief to her nose. Her white wings fluttered with each sneeze.

"I'm so sorry!" she said sadly. "I wanted to make a dignified entrance. . . . It's those dandelions!"

Toby stared at her, astounded.

"I am—*ah-choo!*—Serena, your guardian angel. I'm answering your wish, Toby. You did just call me, didn't you? *Ah-choo!*"

"Yes, I did!" Toby was still stunned by what she was seeing. Her angel had long blonde hair and the most gorgeous ivory gown.

"Toby, I had wanted to wait until I studied you

more before appearing, but a dandelion wish . . . well, I could not ignore that! Here, let me dry those tears."

Serena gently stroked Toby's cheeks, and all her tears disappeared. Her eyes didn't even have that after-crying feeling anymore.

"How did you do that?" Toby asked, amazed.

"Oh, tears are easy!" Serena said casually.

Then Toby couldn't help gushing, "Serena, you are so pretty."

"Well, thank you!" Serena flew around the room a few times, admiring herself in the mirrors.

Then she landed gracefully on the arm of Toby's chair. "I suppose I am," Serena said somewhat immodestly.

"I'm so glad you're here," Toby said eagerly. "I'm in all kinds of trouble."

"I know." Serena's emerald green eyes were sympathetic. "First, let me see that ankle."

Toby carefully took off her shoe. "Ouch!" she yelped.

"Hmm." Serena placed both of her hands on Toby's ankle. Instantly, Toby felt a soft, warm breeze caressing her. The breeze became warmer and her ankle began tingling—and then the pain disappeared!

"I can't believe it!" Toby's eyes went wide. "All the pain is gone."

Toby Takes the Cake

"Of course it is," Serena said confidently. "I got A plus in Sprained Ankles and Wrists at the Angel Academy. Now, try to stand up."

Toby stood up, gingerly putting her weight on her ankle. "It feels fine! As if nothing had ever happened! Oh, Serena, thank you so much!"

"You are perfectly welcome," Serena answered.

Toby tried first position. "No problem!" Second, third, fourth, and fifth were fine, too.

Serena looked extremely relieved. *I haven't made any mistakes so far,* she said to herself.

"Boy," Toby shouted, "if Felicia ever tries anything like that again, I'm going to kill her."

Serena fluttered her wings in alarm. "Oh, I wouldn't do that."

"Don't worry," Toby said quickly, "I'm not *really* going to kill her. That's just an expression. The only thing I've ever punched in my life is a volleyball."

As the angel clock on top of Town Hall began striking six, Serena said, "Uh-oh, I really must go now, but I'm giving you and your family's bakery a lot of thought. In fact, I'm working day and night on your problems. That's easy, of course, since angels never sleep."

"Oh, thank you!" Toby said gratefully. "When are you coming back?"

"Oh, I'm never far away," Serena promised. "I'll be leaving you messages! You can't miss them!"

Toby got excited. "Like the message you wrote on my chocolate cake?"

"Oh, all kinds! Just you wait and see. We angels love surprising people."

Serena waved good-bye and flew angelically out the window, directly back to the Angel Academy to report to Florinda.

"Good work!" Florinda praised Serena. "You appeared just when Toby needed you most."

"And I haven't made one mistake," said Serena, "have I?"

"Well, perhaps one, dear," answered Florinda.

"What?" asked Serena, surprised.

"The mistake about worrying about making mistakes. Remember, Serena, I don't expect you to be a perfect angel!"

"That's right!" Merrie said cheerfully. "*I'm* not! And I did a great job."

Florinda agreed. "Serena, it's quite all right to relax a little! And don't worry so much. Go back and have some fun! Toby could teach you a lot about fun! That's one of the things that makes her your soul mate."

"All right!" Serena promised. She had a lot to think about as she flew back down to earth.

Toby was lying in bed talking to Rachel on the phone. "Guess what!" she said. "I wished on your dandelions, and my angel came! You were right, Rachel! Serena—that's my angel—said she simply had to come when I called her with a dandelion wish."

"Toby, I'm so glad!" Rachel said warmly. "And Serena is such a dreamy name. Did she tumble out of a tree, like Merrie?"

"No!" Toby answered. "She made a perfect landing in my ballet studio. And Rachel, she's *so* graceful . . . more than any dancer I've ever seen!"

"This is so cool!" Rachel shouted. "Now two members of the Angel Club have angels!"

"I'm going to hang up and call Lulu and Val now."

"They'll flip!" Rachel said confidently. "Good night, Toby. See you tomorrow."

"Hey, Lulu, guess what happened?" said Toby when Lulu picked up the phone. "My angel came today."

"No kidding!" Lulu shouted. "That is totally, absolutely supercalifragilisticexpialidocious."

"You've been watching *Mary Poppins* again." Toby laughed.

"Right! Dad's been playing it in the store a lot."

"Serena fixed my sprained ankle," said Toby. "That rotten Felicia tripped me in ballet."

"She's too much!" Lulu said angrily. "We have

to figure out a way to get even with her."

"Let me know if you think of something really good," Toby said. "I have to hang up and call Val now."

"Ta-ta!" Lulu sang, hanging up.

Val's first question was, "What was your angel wearing? Was it a turquoise dress, like Merrie's?"

"No, it was ivory, with spangles and glitter all over. And, oh yes, she had white wings!"

"So elegant!" Val exclaimed. "I'd like to talk more, but I've got to go."

"Bye!" Toby said cheerfully. As she raced downstairs to supper, she told herself, *From now on only great things are going to happen. I just know it!*

Well, great things were definitely being planned at that moment. As soon as Val hung up her phone, it rang again. "Hi," said a familiar voice. "It's Derek Weatherby."

"Hi," Val answered. "How are you?"

"Just fine, Val," Derek said. "Do you remember that research you were doing the other day at the library?"

"Sure I do," Val replied. "But nothing came of it. Lulu and I can't think of anyone who can help Toby continue her lessons."

"Well, that's why I called," Derek said, his voice growing excited. "About an hour ago, Mrs. Heft and her daughter came by my newsstand to pick up copies of *Opera News* and *Dance Today*. And I overheard a conversation they had."

"What was it about?" asked Val eagerly.

"Well, Mrs. Heft was telling Hortense how badly she felt about neglecting the arts in Angel Corners. She mentioned giving money to all kind of groups, but none has anything to do with music or ballet."

"Really?" Val began getting excited. "Maybe Lulu and I can do something about that. Maybe we can ask Mrs. Heft to create a dance scholarship!"

"That's a fine idea," Derek agreed. "May I make a suggestion?"

"Sure! Shoot!"

"Why don't you and Lulu write Mrs. Heft a letter about it?"

"We will!" Val shouted. "That's exactly what we'll do. I'll call Lulu, and we'll write a letter right away."

"Good luck," Derek said. "Let me know how it goes." Then he hung up.

Val called Lulu right away. When she told Lulu all about her idea, Lulu yelled so loudly Val had to hold the phone away from her ear.

"Let's write the note together right now on the phone," Lulu urged. "Then tomorrow, I'll type it up on the computer in our video store."

"You got it!" Val agreed. So that's what they did.

8

Hefty Cakes

The next day was Saturday, when Toby usually worked in the bakery from nine to one. But before she went downstairs, she phoned Madame Maximova to tell her that her ankle was better.

"I'm so relieved, my dear!" Madame said.

Toby hurried into the bakery.

"Morning, Toby." Her mom noticed she was walking normally again. "It looks like your ankle has improved a lot."

"It has!"

"That's wonderful news." Toby's mother kissed her on the cheek, on a freckle. "Did you know freckles are called angel kisses, Toby?"

"I do now!" Toby answered. If only her mother knew that an angel was watching them!

Toby reached for a doughnut—her breakfast. Her dad was pacing, looking worried. "We didn't bake any apple turnovers today. Nobody seems to be buying them."

"This is getting scary," Toby told her parents. "I've never seen so few customers in the bakery. Saturday is usually so busy."

Toby's dad sighed. "Uh-oh, here comes Jerry Beckwith again. There never was a more pesky salesman."

"Howdy-do!" A man in a rumpled raincoat came hurrying in.

"Hello, Mr. Beckwith," answered Mr. Antonio in an almost-patient voice. "Don't bother to show us anything today. We don't need any pie pans or spatulas. Business has been crummy."

"Crummy! That's funny in a bakery! Get it?" Mr. Beckwith had three chins and they all wobbled. "What you *do* need are some of these," he insisted. He opened his big black suitcase and took out some small heart-shaped pans.

"Pretty, huh? They're all the rage on the West Coast."

"No thanks." Toby's dad shook his head.

"But everyone's crazy about them," Mr. Beckwith insisted.

"I told you, we don't need anything," said Toby's dad a little less patiently.

"Okay, okay."

"Here," offered Toby's mom. "Have a cheese Danish." She was feeling sorry for the salesman. He was trying to earn a living, too.

"Thanks!" Mr. Beckwith tipped his hat. After he gulped down the pastry, he looked at his watch. "Uh-oh! I've got to catch the next train! See you!" And he went running out the door.

After he had been gone a few minutes, Toby's mom said, "Oh no, he forgot his heart-shaped pans."

"It's too late to catch him," sighed Mr. Antonio. "The train's already gone. I'll give these back the next time he comes."

"These pans are pretty." Toby picked one up. "There must be some way we can use them."

Just a few minutes later, Helena Heft and her daughter Hortense came in.

"Good morning, Helena. Good morning, Hortense," said Toby's mom.

Mrs. Heft got right down to business. "We need a wedding cake for Hortense's wedding."

"Ah, yes indeed!" Mr. Antonio's face grew cheerful. Wedding cakes were so profitable!

"What can you suggest?" asked Hortense. She was tall, with lovely pale skin and blonde hair.

Toby Takes the Cake

Today—as she did almost every day—she was wearing riding pants and boots.

"Well, how about a yellow cake with hazelnut frosting?"

Mrs. Heft frowned. "I'm sick to death of those. They seem to pop up at every wedding. I want to do something spectacular."

"You're going to be a gorgeous bride!" Toby told Hortense.

"Well, thank you!" Hortense blushed. "I'm a little overwhelmed by it all. I wanted to get married on horseback! You know how wild I am about horses. But Mom wants a big formal thing."

"Let me think," Toby's mother was telling Mrs. Heft. "How about a black forest cake? It's filled with chocolate and cherries."

"Luscious!" Mrs. Heft said, but then she shook her head. "But too rich. Everybody I know is on a diet."

"But a wedding is a special occasion," Mr. Antonio insisted.

"I know," Mrs. Heft agreed, "but everyone is scared of cholesterol."

Toby remembered the research she'd done with Rachel. Cholesterol was as bad for humans as Kryptonite was for Superman.

"Maybe we should skip the cake and serve fresh fruit instead," Mrs. Heft told Hortense. As Toby's parents started to protest, Mrs. Heft headed toward the door, with her daughter in tow.

Suddenly, a huge cookbook tumbled off the shelf, landing on the floor with a thud. As Toby picked it up, she noticed that the book was opened to a recipe for angel food cake. Toby heard a small voice in her ear. It was Serena! "Read the recipe!" the angel whispered. Toby scanned it quickly.

"Look!" she said, rushing over to Mrs. Heft. "Here's a cake that's made without egg yolks, or cream, or butter."

Mrs. Heft read the recipe. "That's true, but wouldn't a plain angel food cake look . . . well . . . dull?"

"Oh no!" said Mr. Antonio quickly. "We'll decorate it! Of course, not with butter cream frosting. But we'll think of something."

"I'm sorry." Mrs. Heft shook her head. "It just sounds so ordinary. Doesn't it, Hortense? We need something more romantic. Something with hearts and flowers." Mrs. Heft began walking toward the door again.

Clang! One of the heart-shaped pans fell off the shelf! It was Serena again!

Toby picked up the pan. "Look at this!" she said quickly. "It's the latest rage on the West Coast— and very romantic! Why don't we bake lots of tiny heart-shaped angel food cakes, and place them around the huge angel food wedding cake? It would be very dramatic! And your guests can take the little cakes home!"

"Now, that's a charming idea!" responded Mrs. Heft. Hortense was delighted, too. "Could you make a hundred of them?" Mrs. Heft asked.

"Easy as pie!" Mr. Antonio's eyes twinkled at the thought of so many.

"Madeline McWithers will be sick with envy!" Mrs. Heft said. "It's a deal, Mr. Antonio. Let me write you a check for the deposit right now."

Mr. Antonio grabbed his calculator. The price of Mrs. Heft's cakes turned out to be nice and hefty.

"It's worth every penny," she crooned. "It will be so charming!"

Hortense whispered in Toby's ear, "Thanks so much for thinking of it! Mom would've dragged me to every bakery on the East Coast if you hadn't." Then she resumed her normal voice. "How is your ballet coming? I saw you dancing by Angel Stream the other day."

"Um . . ." Toby said. "It's great, really, but I have to stop taking ballet next semester."

"Really? That's awful! Why is that?" Hortense asked, but before Toby could answer, Mrs. Heft was tugging at her daughter's arm. "Come, dear, it's on to Petak's Florist for flower selection."

As soon as the two women were gone, Toby's

dad rushed over to give his daughter a big hug. "Good going!" he boomed in his deep voice. "And you're not grounded anymore!"

Toby's mom was so pleased, she danced a little jig. "These wedding cakes could be the shot in the arm our bakery needs. When people taste them, they'll be lining up to buy our cakes again!"

"Right," said Toby's dad. "Isn't it odd how that cookbook fell off the shelf at just the right moment? And that heart-shaped pan, too?"

Toby didn't say a word, but silently she thanked Serena.

"Life is filled with surprises," said Mr. Antonio. "I sort of like it that way."

"So do we!" agreed Amber, as she and Merrie and Celeste watched them from the Angel Academy. "Come on," Amber told her friends, "we're late for Serenity Study Hall."

"I'm glad Serena finally *did* something!" sang Celeste as the angels flew through campus together. "And tossing that book off the shelf and that pan! It was so wonderfully dramatic!"

"Yes it was!" Merrie cheered. "Serena is definitely loosening up!"

The angels landed in the central courtyard of the Angel Academy to check out the Bountiful Bulletin Board for extracurricular activities.

"Hmm," noticed Amber, "there's a field trip to all seven heavens. Does anyone want to go?"

"I do!" Celeste answered eagerly.

"Not me!" Merrie replied. "Serena just discovered what I've known for months: Earth is the best fun of all!" And Merrie went flying back down to keep an eye on her charge, Rachel, *and* Serena— skipping study hall altogether!

9

Very Moving Movies

"**R**achel!" Toby was up in her room, on the phone. "I have to tell everyone what Serena just did! Let's have an Angel Club meeting right now."

"I can't," Rachel answered. "I'm helping Mom with a litter of sick rabbits. I'll be working until three o'clock."

"Let's have it then. I'll call Val and Lulu."

Val was nearly hysterical when she heard about the heart-shaped pans falling down. "I want to hear every detail. I should be finished cleaning out my closet by three. Do you need any blouses or skirts? Mom sent me some from Rome, but they mailed the wrong sizes. They're teensy."

"No thanks," Toby said. "I'm bigger than you, remember?"

"Of course! Sorry, Toby. See you later."

Lulu had bad news for Toby. "I can't come. I'm helping Dad at the video store till five. . . . Wait a sec. I have an idea."

Lulu put her hand over the receiver. All Toby heard was "*mumble,* Toby, *mumble, mumble,* Angel Club," then a low voice, which was Mr. Bliss saying, "*mumble,* Lulu, *mumble, mumble.*"

Then Lulu was back. "Good news! Dad said we could have the meeting at our store. But while we're meeting, I'll have to keep an eye on things."

"We'll help you!" Toby promised. "Bye."

Rachel and Val were already at Starlight Video, nibbling popcorn from the machine, when Toby came in. Thanks to the popcorn, you could always smell Starlight Video long before you could see it.

"Tell us everything!" Lulu demanded. She was behind the counter wearing a shocking pink blouse and skirt, and a baseball cap that said MOVIES ARE MY LIFE.

"Lulu, don't you look *gorgeous,*" Toby complimented her. "You too, Val. . . ." Val's red hair was up in a ponytail, and she wore a peach-colored tunic with matching leggings and sneakers. "You're not by any chance expecting Zeb Burgess to stop in for a video or anything, are you?"

"I'm over him!" Val insisted, but she blushed.

"Don't *I* look glamorous, too?" Rachel teased Toby.

Toby grinned at her best friend, who, as usual, wore blue jeans and a T-shirt. Rachel dressed a lot like Toby—for comfort.

"Pull up a few of those stools," Lulu said. "I'm calling this meeting to order so Toby can tell us about her angel. So far, almost all I know is that her name is Serena."

"That's right." Toby took over. She told about the dandelions, and about Serena floating into her room, sneezing. She described how Serena had healed her sprained ankle and then how she knocked down the book and the cake pan in the bakery just when Helena and Hortense Heft were almost out the door.

"So that's how you get an angel!" Lulu jumped up, excited. "You blow on some dandelions! I'll try that tonight."

"Don't bother!" Rachel said. "It's obvious that each angel comes in her own way."

"I hate it when you act like such a know-it-all!" Lulu snapped.

"Sorry," Rachel apologized.

"I'll tell you something cute about my angel,"

Toby said, and giggled. "She sure likes looking at herself in the mirror."

As Toby spoke, *plop!* a video fell off the shelf. It was *Angel Face.*

"Serena, that was you, wasn't it?" Toby looked up at the shelf.

"Of course!" Serena was suddenly there, hovering between the aisles.

"Where is she?" asked Lulu eagerly.

Toby pointed. "She's landing on top of the popcorn machine."

"It's so warm and cozy up here," Serena crooned.

"Oh, I wish I could see her! It's so maddening!" Lulu complained.

"Me, too," Rachel said. "But you know the rules. You only can see your own guardian angel, nobody else's."

"We *know*, Rachel, we *know!*" said Lulu.

"Sorry!" exclaimed Rachel.

"Ask Serena what she thinks of us," Val told Toby.

There was a short pause.

Then, *plop!* another movie fell off the shelf: *Angels in Disguise.*

Everyone laughed.

"Ask Serena what her favorite movie is," urged Lulu.

Plop! Angels in the Outfield fell off the shelf.

Everyone was amused except Lulu's dad, who came in from the back of the store. "What's going on here? Why are these videotapes on the floor?"

"Uh . . . sorry," Lulu answered, quickly picking up the videos and putting them back where they belonged.

"Listen, Lulu," said her father, "I need a break and a cup of coffee. Watch the store for a few minutes, okay?"

Lulu's almond eyes narrowed. "You're not having coffee with Ms. Swift, the librarian, are you?" Lulu was very possessive of her dad. He had been Lulu's whole family since her mother died when she was a baby.

"No, I'm not," he declared, then rumpled his daughter's hair and walked out the door.

Serena made a mental note to tell Florinda: That man definitely needs a soul mate. "Um, Toby, I've never attended an Angel Club meeting on earth before. Do you mind if I stay and watch?"

"Of course you can stay!" Toby assured her.

Rachel asked, "Is there any more business for the Angel Club?"

"Yes!" Lulu piped up. "I'm furious that Felicia tried to hurt Toby. I think we should do something to get even with her."

"Like what?" Toby asked.

"Well, I was thinking," said Lulu, her eyes twinkling, "Felicia tripped Toby because she wanted to dance the lead role in *The Firebird*, right? So let's fool her into believing that her trick worked!"

"How do we do that?" asked Rachel.

"Here's how: Toby, on Monday when you come to school, pretend your ankle still hurts. Limp around and look pathetic. Then when Felicia goes to ballet class, she'll think the role is hers. But, when the *Firebird* rehearsal starts, you can have a sudden recovery. Felicia will be stunned!"

Val's violet eyes lit up. "Lulu, you have the mind of a first-class villain."

"When I get angry at someone, I never let up!" Lulu said furiously. "Besides, Felicia deserves it."

"I'll do it!" Toby agreed. "And I'll give the Angel Club a full report on Felicia's reaction!"

Just then, Hortense Heft came into the store to return a videotape. She was wearing her riding outfit again.

"I was watching *Father of the Bride* last night," Hortense explained. "I needed to relax a little. My wedding is making me as nervous as an untrained pony." Then she turned to Toby. "I'm sorry I won't be at your dance recital. I'll be on my honeymoon."

"That's okay," Toby assured her.

"I'll videotape it for you," Lulu offered.

"Thanks so much! Bye, girls," Hortense said, about to leave. "See you at the wedding!"

"Um, Hortense, can I speak to you for a second?" Val said quickly.

"Me, too!" Lulu jumped up.

They both went into a corner with Hortense. After whispering for a while, Val handed Hortense an envelope. She nodded, put it into her purse, and left the store.

"What was that all about?" Toby asked.

"Um . . ." began Val, "all I can say right now is that Lulu and I are working on a way for you to keep up your ballet lessons—"

"Oh, Val!" Toby moaned.

"There's nothing to worry about," Lulu added quickly. "Our project doesn't involve the newspaper or anyone knowing about the bakery's troubles. We can't say any more, Toby. But just keep your fingers crossed that everything will turn out okay."

"Is there any more Angel Club business?" Rachel asked.

"Well," said Val quietly, "I don't really know if this is official business, but lately, I've been noticing that Andrea's clothes are sort of worn out. I was thinking I would give her some of the clothes Mom sent me from Rome. They'd fit her perfectly."

"That's a nice idea." Lulu squeezed her hand.

"Andrea and Sylvie are friends again," Toby said, with a smile. "I saw them together at the sweet shop having lemonade."

Toby Takes the Cake

"I'm so glad," Rachel said. "Well, I guess if there's no more business, I'll adjourn this meeting."

All the girls got up to go. Serena flew over and whispered in Toby's ear, "Your Angel Club meeting was so remarkable, Toby. I can't wait to tell my friends about it."

"What do you mean?" Toby asked.

"You'd be surprised how few people on earth really take the time to help one another the way you girls do!"

Serena flew off, calling back over her shoulder, "I'll be back, Toby! You can count on that!"

10

Ankles Away!

On Monday, Toby remembered to limp to class. When Felicia saw her, she said, "I'm so sorry your ankle still hurts. I'd better bring my *Firebird* ballet costume to class today. Madame Maximova may want to choose another soloist."

"Oh gosh, I hope not." Toby pretended to be stricken.

Later, at lunch, Toby told all the members of the Angel Club how well their plan was going.

"How I wish I could see Felicia's face when you start dancing!" whooped Val. "I'll be back in a sec. I have a little errand to run." Val left the table and carried a bulging backpack over to where Andrea was sitting. She whispered something to Andrea, and they both headed to the girls' bathroom.

When they came back, Andrea had a bulging backpack and a cheerful expression on her face. Val looked pretty happy, too.

She came back and sat down with the Angel Club. "Andrea loves the clothes. I told her it was like a loan, so she wouldn't be embarrassed. And I said when she outgrew them, she could give them to somebody else."

"Nice work!" Toby said.

Val continued, "Andrea said she and Sylvie are good friends now. She even invited Sylvie over to her house today to see her prize rabbit. Remember how cute he was at Founders Day? He won a ribbon."

"I'm really glad things are better for Andrea," Toby said.

What Toby didn't know was that things were about to change—in a terrible way!

On her way to ballet class, still limping in case Felicia saw her, Toby passed Rachel's house. Rachel was out in front on Rollerblades and Andrea was on roller skates.

And, suddenly, Sylvie was there, too, shouting, with her hands on her hips. "Andrea, you lied to me! You promised I could come to your house today!

But then you said I couldn't because you had to go to the doctor. So how come you're here skating with Rachel?" Sylvie looked terribly hurt.

"I— I—" Andrea began, and then she couldn't say anything. She chewed on one of her braids, staring down at the sidewalk.

"I hate you, Andrea!" Sylvie yelled. "And I'm never speaking to you again." She turned around and stomped away.

"What's going on?" Toby asked Andrea. "Why are you skating with Rachel instead of having Sylvie come over to your house?"

"Um, I'm not actually skating with Rachel." Andrea looked away, answering in a wispy voice. "I only skated over to return her book, *Harriet the Spy.*"

"That's right," Rachel joined in. "I just happened to be skating when Andrea came by."

"Andrea, I don't mean to be nosy, but why didn't you keep your date with Sylvie?" Toby asked.

Andrea's pale face flushed with embarrassment. "The thing is . . . I invited Sylvie to my house . . . to see my rabbit. . . . But when I thought about what my house is like, I started to worry."

"What's wrong with your house?" Toby asked.

"It's not the house, exactly. It's my dad. He still can't find a job, and sometimes he gets so grumpy and depressed. I thought if Sylvie met him, he might scare her, and she wouldn't want to be my friend anymore. Felicia keeps telling me people won't like me if they meet my dad. That's why I lied to Sylvie and told her I had a doctor's appointment."

Toby was furious. "Felicia is just trying to scare you so you'll be her friend again."

"But you should see my dad!" Andrea insisted. "He can be so awful!"

"My father and my brothers get angry, too, sometimes," Toby explained. "They get loud, too, but then it passes . . . and everything's okay again."

"That's different from my house. My dad is much worse." Andrea shook her head. "Listen . . . I've got to go." She skated away.

Rachel and Toby shared a determined look. "We are not giving up yet!" Rachel said.

"No way!" Toby insisted. "But right now, I have to go. I'll be late for class if I don't hurry."

As soon as Toby walked into the dressing room, Sasha asked her, "How's your ankle? Is it better?"

"Not so great." Toby crossed her fingers when she said it.

Felicia came in just then. She changed into a leotard covered with tiny red beads and feathers. "This is my *Firebird* costume," she bragged. "Isn't it delicious? By the way, how is your ankle?"

"Awful!" Toby suppressed a smirk as she

changed into her tights and leotard. Then she put up her braid and limped to class.

She took her place at the barre and pretended to have trouble with her warm-ups.

Madame Maximova came in and put on a record.

As the music began, Toby heard a light voice humming along. It was Serena's. "I wouldn't miss this for the world!" she whispered.

The class began doing exercises at the barre. Felicia kept glancing at Toby when she wasn't admiring her own costume in the mirror.

"Now, Toby," said Madame Maximova, "try your solo. Let's see how your ankle is doing."

"I don't think it's any better," Felicia piped up.

"Let me be the judge of that," said Madame Maximova sternly. "And whatever is that you are wearing, Felicia? You know the dress code! We will discuss this later." She put on the wild *Firebird* music.

Toby began slowly, as if her ankle still hurt. "I think it's warming up," she said, gazing at Felicia. And then Toby burst into a long series of leaps and pirouettes!

Felicia's eyes went wide, and she frowned. "What's going on? I thought you said your ankle still hurt."

"I guess an angel must have fixed it or something!" Toby said gleefully.

Felicia leaped up and rushed over to Madame Maximova. "Toby played a trick on me! That's not fair! She pretended her ankle hurt and it didn't! You should take the role away from her and give it to me. That's why I wore my costume, and I can jump much higher than Toby!"

Felicia did a quick jump. Too quick—because she didn't watch her leg position. She stumbled and fell down.

"Oh, Felicia," Madame Maximova said sadly, "when will you ever learn the importance of controlled movement and practice?" She walked over and extended a hand to help her up.

Felicia refused her help. "I hate ballet!" she shouted. "It's stupid!" And she got up and stalked out of the room.

The whole class was shocked into silence. Then somebody laughed, and everyone else did, too.

"Let's get back to work," said Madame Maximova. "Toby, I think you are going to be splendid at the recital. And to make it a very special night, I want to lend you a costume I wore as a girl in Moscow. My mother wore it, too, when she was a girl."

Madame Maximova opened a large box and

took out a red and gold costume all covered with feathers.

"It's gorgeous," Toby gasped. "Are you sure you want me to wear it?"

"I'm sure!" insisted Madame Maximova. "A ballet dress only comes to life when someone is dancing in it."

Toby hugged the costume close. "I'll take extra-good care of it," she promised.

"Now, then, dancers," Madame Maximova announced, "as you leave today, pick up your recital tickets for your family and friends. Take as many as you think you can use."

Toby counted up the number she needed for her parents and brothers and for her friends in the Angel Club. Then she got a sudden inspiration and added two more tickets. *Wait'll I tell Rachel my idea!* Toby thought.

When Toby got home, she took a shower and put on the *Firebird* costume. "Wow!" she said, gazing at herself in the mirror. "I look like a real ballerina."

"You look lovely!" Serena was suddenly there beside her.

Toby spun around and gave her a hug.

"I came to help you rehearse your role," said Serena. "But first, I'd like to show you a special way to put up your hair."

Toby sat down on the armchair, and Serena

brushed Toby's hair and then pinned it up in a pretty swirl.

"It's so elegant!" Toby said.

"I should hope so." Serena smiled. She walked to the piano stool and sat down, arranging her ivory dress neatly around her, as if she were about to give a concert.

Then Serena tucked her wings close and began playing the music for Toby's solo.

"Go ahead," she said gently, "dance, Toby! I'll play the music for as long as you need to practice."

"Great! Thanks!" Toby practiced for quite a while.

"I'm not sure you got that last leap right," Serena noticed. She got up from the piano stool, but the music kept playing!

Serena placed her arm around Toby's waist and helped her achieve a higher elevation. "Much better!" she declared.

She kept her eye on Toby while she practiced.

And when the sun went down over Angel Corners that night, Toby was still dancing, with the heavenly support of her guardian angel.

CHAPTER

11

Angels of Mercy

Before she went to bed that night, Toby called Rachel. "Listen," Toby said. "I've come up with a plan to help Andrea and Sylvie get together again."

"What's your plan?" Rachel asked eagerly.

"I'll tell you tomorrow!"

At lunch the next day, Toby saw Andrea and Sylvie sitting at different tables. Each of them was pretending to read a book while she was eating, but Toby noticed that neither girl ever turned the pages.

"Here's my plan," Toby told her friends in the Angel Club. "I'm going to give Andrea and Sylvie tickets for my ballet recital." She giggled. "The seats are right next to each other!"

"That's clever!" Val said. "If they sit together, sooner or later, one of them will break down, and they'll have to make up."

"I agree." Lulu nodded. "But how will we be sure that Sylvie and Andrea show up? What if they decide to stay home?"

"Um, I didn't think of that," confessed Toby.

"I know what to do!" said Rachel. "Let's go to their houses before the recital and pick them up. I'll go to Andrea's, and Val and Lulu can go to Sylvie's."

"Oh, we're so clever!" Lulu said happily. "Someone should make a movie about us."

"I'll go give Sylvie her ticket now," Toby decided. She casually walked over to Sylvie's table and said, "Hey, Sylvie, would you like to come to my dance recital next week? I have an extra ticket for you."

"Really? You want *me* to come?" Sylvie's dark eyes shone.

"Yes, I do," Toby said sincerely. "Sylvie, I'd feel a lot better knowing the audience was full of friendly faces. Will you come?"

"All right." Sylvie nodded shyly. "It'll sure beat staying home and watching TV."

"Oh, it will be a lot more fun!" Toby answered. "I think the evening will prove to be *very* dramatic."

Later that afternoon, Toby ran up to Andrea, who was heading home, and gave her a ticket, too.

"I'll try to come," Andrea said, "but my dad might not let me. Sometimes he feels so bad when people give us things that he won't let us have them."

"But this ticket is free. Nobody pays for it," Toby reminded Andrea.

"I'll tell Dad that," Andrea promised. "I haven't gone anywhere in such a long time."

"Rachel will come by and pick you up," Toby added. "I have to be there early to warm up."

Everything went smoothly for the rest of the week. Toby rehearsed her part with the corps, and Madame Maximova was very pleased with her progress.

On Friday, when Toby got home from her lesson, she hurried to the bakery to tell her mother how well things were going.

"Where's Mom?" Toby asked her dad. "She's usually baking muffins now."

Her father sighed. "Your mom has come down with the flu. She's upstairs in bed."

"Poor Mom!"

"Why don't you take her some chamomile tea, Toby. I'm sure she'd appreciate that."

"Sure, Dad." As Toby was putting on the kettle, she noticed a worried expression flicker across her dad's face.

Toby Takes the Cake

"There couldn't be a worse time for your mom to get sick. We have to start baking the angel food wedding cakes tomorrow. I was counting on her help."

"Let *me* help," Toby offered.

"No way!" Her dad shook his head. "Not after what you did to that sourdough bread."

"Dad!" Toby said fiercely. "Will you *ever* forgive me for that?"

He shrugged with a smile that meant "maybe," but said, "I'm certainly not going to trust you with this project. It's too important."

Toby tried every argument she could think of to convince her dad, but he refused to change his mind.

When Toby brought tea up to her mom, she found her wrapped up in so many blankets, she looked like a mummy. "What an awful time to get sick!" Mrs. Antonio whispered in a hoarse voice. "Both your brothers are away for the weekend, so they can't help your dad bake."

"If only he'd let *me* help," Toby said sadly. "I want to so badly."

Mrs. Antonio shivered as she sipped the tea. "Ouch! My head is killing me."

"Rest now," Toby told her mother, "and call me if there's anything you need. I'm going up to the attic to practice my solo."

Toby put on Madame Maximova's beautiful

dress. She fixed her hair the way that Serena had shown her. Then she put on a tape of Stravinsky's *Firebird* and began to dance.

Toby decided to improvise with a few fancier steps. She did a deep plié and then another. After that she began spinning around the room faster and faster.

Then Toby flung out her arms as far as she could and leaped!

Suddenly, she heard a terrible *rrrrrrip!*

"Oh no!" The *Firebird* costume had torn all along the seam! The rip stretched from her armpit down to her waist, and feathers were flying all over the place. Toby tried to snatch them up, but it was like trying to catch handfuls of air!

"I can't believe I did such a careless thing! What am I going to do? If Mom weren't sick, she could fix this for me, but I can't bother her with it now."

As Toby gazed at the dress helplessly, she wondered if Serena could help her.

"Here I am!" Serena appeared in a swirl of gold light. "But . . . um, Toby . . . I'm a little embarrassed about this," said her angel. "I know I *should* be able to mend this dress, but I can't."

Toby's face fell. "I thought angels could do anything."

"Not quite," said Serena sadly. "I have to confess something: I wasn't paying attention when we studied the design and care of heavenly and earthly attire. I was too busy trying on all the different gowns."

Toby couldn't help smiling. Then she said, "I'll think of something. . . . At least, I hope I will."

That night Toby had a hard time falling asleep. She wondered just how—or whether—Madame Maximova's costume could ever be mended.

12

Toby Gets Her Chance

The next morning, when Toby came downstairs, she found her father standing at the bakery counter, wrapped in a blanket.

He shivered and groaned. "I think I have the flu," he said.

"Not you, too!" Toby had never seen her dad's face look so pale. "Go back to bed!" she urged him. "You shouldn't be down here at all with your germs."

Mr. Antonio leaned against the counter, wiping his perspiring face with a towel. "Uh-oh, I think I'm going to faint."

Toby gasped. She didn't know what to do. "Please, Dad, I think you should go back to bed."

Toby Takes the Cake

She reached out to him. "I'll help you walk upstairs."

"I can't leave the bakery," Mr. Antonio insisted. "I have to bake Mrs. Heft's wedding cakes. Tomorrow's Sunday! It's the wedding! If I don't deliver one hundred and one cakes, our bakery's reputation will be ruined." Mr. Antonio wiped his brow again and then collapsed onto a chair.

Toby's heart was pounding with worry. "Dad, please go back to bed. You're so weak, you can't even stand up."

"I guess I have no choice," Mr. Antonio groaned. "But first, I'll call Mrs. Heft and tell her I can't bake her cakes."

"No, don't!" Toby said fiercely. "Let *me* bake them. I've baked lots of cakes."

Toby's dad shook his head. "It's too big a job!"

Toby was nearly in tears. "But if we don't do it, everyone in Angel Corners will say you let the Hefts down. Then nobody will trust us with their party orders! Dad, don't you always tell us that families should stick together? So why don't you let me help you?"

Her father looked at her for a long moment. Then he said wearily, "I do say that all the time. I guess I should give you a chance. All right then, Toby. If you want to bake the cakes you might as well try."

"Right!" Toby raised her fist in triumph. Then she gulped. *Am I really up to this?* she wondered.

As Mr. Antonio turned to go, he said, "Come upstairs later, and I'll go over the recipe with you. You'll have to do the baking tonight, because you'll be selling bread all day."

"I'll call up my friends in the Angel Club," Toby decided. "They can help me. It's Saturday night, so we can all stay up late."

"You're my girl," Mr. Antonio said softly. "It's time I showed some faith in you."

"Right!" Toby couldn't agree more.

After her dad was gone, Toby's heart began to pound again like mad. "I've never baked an angel food cake in my life. And I've got to do a hundred and one of them—perfectly!"

She grabbed an apron. "Hey!" Her face lit up as she saw red embroidered script begin to appear on the apron, spelling out:

World's Greatest Angel Food Cake Baker!

"Serena, I hope you're right."

"Of course I'm right!" Serena said playfully. She landed on the scales. Toby noticed that she weighed nothing.

"I'll be here to help you," Serena promised.

Toby wondered if her guardian angel had paid

any attention in baking class, but she was much too worried to ask!

Toby grabbed the phone and called all her friends in the Angel Club.

"I'll be there!" Rachel promised. "I'll help you beat the egg whites. My arms are stronger now, from lots of basketball playing!"

Val said, "I'll bring some cake decorating books along. Mom got them in Italy."

"Hey, Val," Toby remembered, "I tore my *Firebird* costume and all the feathers went flying off. Do you know anyone who can fix it?"

"No, I don't," Val said. "Ms. Strack, the best seamstress in Angel Corners, is on vacation in Mexico. Mom made all her reservations at the travel agency."

"Drat!" Toby groaned. Then she hung up and phoned Lulu.

Lulu was very excited. "I'm going to help bake Hortense's wedding cake? Cool! Let's make it really special. And I'll bring my Minicam just in case Serena does something wild tonight! Maybe I can capture her on tape!"

"Lulu Bliss, don't you dare!" Toby ordered. "This kitchen is going to be busy enough without you running around with your camera. You're sure to knock over a cake!"

"Okay, okay! Calm down," Lulu muttered. "See you at six."

All day long, Toby was a nervous wreck. Even though there weren't many customers, she was relieved when the time came to close up the shop.

Finally, at six o'clock, her friends arrived.

"Look at my apron!" said Toby. They all looked at it blankly. "Oh, I forgot, you can't see Serena's writing. Well, it says 'World's Greatest Angel Food Cake Baker!' and that's what I intend to be."

"I love it, even if I can't see it," said Val. Val wore a fancy apron, too. It said 'Parisian Cooking School' on it, with a picture of the Eiffel Tower.

Lulu was wearing a painter's apron with lots of pockets. "Dad got it at a flea market," Lulu explained. "Oh, and I have a surprise. I'll show it to you later." She stuck a shopping bag in the corner.

Toby rolled her eyes. "I don't think I can take too many more surprises!"

Rachel came in wearing jeans and an old striped shirt that had belonged to her dad. It was so big on her that it came down past her knees. But Rachel loved it because it reminded her of him.

"Okay," Toby began, "I went over the recipe with Dad, and he said the first thing to do is to set out everything we need." She opened the cupboard and took out huge sacks of sugar and flour. She put the flour on the shelf above the table. "The eggs are already at room temperature," she said. She got out the lemon juice and the cream of tartar, too.

"I love those tiny heart-shaped pans," said Val. "They're dreamy. I'm going to use them at my own wedding."

"To Zeb Burgess?" Lulu teased.

"Who else?" Val said proudly. "He winked at me today when he walked by."

"No he didn't!" Lulu insisted. "He had something in his eye! I was with you, remember?"

Toby began washing off the counter. "Dad said everything has to be immaculately clean!"

"Maybe you should use some more soap," Serena suggested.

"All right," Toby spoke to the ceiling.

"Serena must be here," declared Lulu. "Toby's talking to the air again."

"I'll stay invisible so I won't distract you," Serena told Toby.

"Good idea!" Toby answered. She opened the cupboard and took out a stack of big angel food cake pans for the layers of the big cake.

"Be careful," Serena shouted in Toby's ear. "You don't want to drop them!"

Well, Toby was so startled, she did drop them! "Now I have to wash them again!"

"I'm sorry!" Serena apologized.

"You're making me nervous!" Toby told her. "Please stop hovering around."

"But that's my job!" Serena said. Still, she backed off a bit.

Rachel volunteered to wash the pans.

"And I'll dry them," Lulu offered.

"Thanks." Toby began opening crates of eggs. "I'll start separating the yolks and the whites. We only need whites for the cake."

"No yoking!" teased Lulu, from the sink.

"Whites in one bowl, yolks in the other," Toby chanted to herself.

One yolk broke and a tiny bit got into the whites, but Toby didn't notice it right away.

Serena couldn't resist flying down to warn her about it. "Uh-oh!" She bumped into a sack of flour on the shelf above the table. It tipped over, and flour poured out—all over Toby.

"You look like Robin Williams in *Mrs. Doubtfire!*" Lulu laughed.

Toby wanted to cry. "It's not funny! Everything's going wrong." She went into the bathroom to wash herself off.

Serena was horrified. "I can't believe I *did* that! Some guardian angel *I* am!" She went and sat in the corner, vowing not to make one more move unless Toby really needed her.

CHAPTER

13

One Hundred and One Angel Food Cakes!

A few minutes later, things were under control again. Toby had calmed down. Rachel had removed the bit of egg yolk from the whites and reminded her they had plenty of flour left and no great harm had been done.

Val set up the electric mixers, and she and Toby began beating the egg whites, adding a little cream of tartar.

"Rachel and Lulu, you can sift the flour and sugar," Toby said.

"The book says we have to sift the flour four times," noted Lulu. "Once by itself, and three times with the sugar."

"And don't cheat!" Rachel told her. "I'm watching."

"*Moi?*" Lulu giggled.

"Did you preheat the oven?" Val asked Toby.

"Yes, to three hundred and fifty degrees. But thanks for asking, Val."

After the egg whites were stiff, Toby added the vanilla and almond extracts. Then she sifted the sugar-flour mixture onto them and folded it in gently with a rubber spatula. "The first batch is ready to go into the oven now," she said, wiping her forehead with a towel.

Toby carefully poured the batter into the angel food pans and set them in the oven. "Let us pray," she intoned, setting the timer for forty-five minutes.

While the first batch of cakes was baking, the girls began the next batch.

Soon the kitchen began to be filled with a sweet aroma.

"Yum," Lulu said. "Do we get samples?"

"Only if there are extra cakes," Toby said. "Which I doubt."

Val asked, "Does everyone know how Hortense met her fiancé?"

"It's a funny story!" Lulu chimed in. "Hortense was at a horse show, and a man was tossed from his horse. Hortense rushed over and picked him up, and it was love at first sight! He was lying with a bump on his head in a bed of red tulips."

"How romantic!" Val gushed. Then she said, "I have to go upstairs for a minute. I'll be right back."

Soon the first batch of cakes was ready to come out of the oven.

"They're beautiful," Rachel said, excited. "Now we have only a million batches to go!"

"Tall and light as a feather!" Toby said. "So far, so good. Now, let's check out frosting recipes." Toby began studying a cookbook. "Uh-oh," she said nervously. "All of these recipes are loaded with butter and cream. And we promised Mrs. Heft we wouldn't use any."

Toby looked around helplessly. None of her friends had a solution. And where was Val? She was still upstairs somewhere.

A small light voice from the corner said, "Um, Toby, I think I can help you."

"Serena!" Toby ran over to her. "How?"

"I can go up to the Celestial Cafeteria. Our chef has a great recipe for cake frosting. It's absolutely heavenly, and it hasn't one harmful ingredient."

"Serena, you'll be saving my life!" said Toby, relieved.

"It's my pleasure," Serena answered. "I'll be right back."

While her guardian angel was gone, Toby put more cakes into the oven.

Val returned from upstairs, holding something behind her back.

"Where have you been?" Toby asked. "And what are you hiding?"

"Look!" Val's face lit up. And she handed Toby the *Firebird* costume perfectly repaired.

"How did you do that?" Toby asked, after giving Val a huge hug.

"It's very simple. Mom knew where Ms. Strack, the seamstress, was staying in Mexico, so she let me call her and ask how to fix the costume. I went upstairs to put on the finishing touches."

"My friends are all geniuses!" Toby declared.

"Did someone say genius?" It was Serena, back with a large golden bowl filled with frosting.

Lulu and Val stared, amazed, at a bowl floating in midair.

"It looks like regular frosting," commented Toby.

"But it's not!" Serena assured her. "Earth has never seen—or tasted—anything like it, until now!"

Toby grabbed a spatula and began spreading the frosting on a cake. "It's so smooth!"

"Let me do a cake!" begged Lulu.

"There are plenty of cakes for all of us to do," Toby told her.

So all the girls got spatulas and dipped them into Serena's golden bowl of frosting. The bowl kept refilling, never running out, as cake after cake was covered.

"Now let's do the decorations," Toby said. "Can anyone draw roses? I never watched when Mom wanted to teach me."

"Just like me and sewing class!" Serena whispered in Toby's ear.

Val tried to squeeze a rose out of the pastry tube, but only a blob came out.

"Let me try," Rachel offered. She made a bigger blob.

Lulu made a few blobs and gave up.

"Why is it so hard to do?" Toby wondered. "It's just like fancy handwriting."

"Um-hmm!" Serena suddenly cleared her throat.

"Serena!" Toby remembered. "You have gorgeous handwriting. Will you help us decorate the cakes?"

"I was just waiting for you to ask." Serena beamed. "Let me have that pastry tube."

Val, Rachel, and Lulu saw the pastry tube leave Toby's hands and go flying into the air. Then they watched it point down toward the large cake.

Serena drew a row of red tulips around the edge.

"I get it!" Toby guessed. "Those are the red tulips Vic fell into when Hortense saved him!"

"That's right. It was a match made in Heaven."

Serena smiled as she added green stems and leaves.

In a few minutes, she had finished each of the layers of the large cake.

"What shall we put on the small heart-shaped cakes?" asked Toby.

"I know," Serena said. She drew angels' wings in the middle of each cake.

"Serena, you are incredible!" Toby said. Her friends felt the same way.

"Oh, it's nothing!" Serena said modestly, but she was thrilled with herself.

Toby went to a cupboard and took out the bride and groom dolls for the top of the cake.

"Wait!" Lulu shook her head. "I have something better. It's time to reveal my surprise." Lulu grabbed the shopping bag she'd brought with her and reached inside. She took out plastic dolls of a bride and groom on horseback.

"They're perfect!" Toby squealed.

Lulu agreed. "My father found them at a movie auction. They were on a wedding cake in a Western movie. They're only on loan, you know!"

"Sure, sure!" Toby said.

They all stood silently admiring the cake. "I wish Mom and Dad could see it," Toby said wistfully.

"Um, I can help you there, too," Lulu piped up again. "I brought my Polaroid."

Toby Takes the Cake

"Lu-*lu!* Lu-*lu!*" Toby cheered. Rachel and Val joined in.

Lulu snapped four quick pictures of Toby with the cake. "Now each of us can have a photo."

"I'm going to put it in the frame with my Angel Club picture," Rachel decided.

"I'll be back in a sec," Toby said. She ran upstairs and showed the photo to her parents.

"The cake is gorgeous!" said Mrs. Antonio.

"You performed a miracle!" her dad said, beaming. "Congratulations!"

"That means a lot, coming from you," Toby told him, and then she went back downstairs. "We have a lot more work to do," she told her friends. "Let's get going."

Rachel started separating egg yolks from the whites. Val picked up the sifter as Lulu measured cream of tartar. Serena drew wings, and Toby supervised.

As they worked, Rachel told them that Andrea and Sylvie were still not speaking to each other. "I hope our ticket plan for the recital works," she said.

"I know it will work!" Toby insisted. "I noticed the two of them glancing at each other in class yesterday. They just need a little push."

Hours later, when Lulu's dad came to pick up the girls, Toby thanked them over and over. "You're the best friends in the world!"

After Val, Lulu, and Rachel had gone, Serena flew over to Toby in a blaze of golden light.

"Oh, Serena!" Toby said as she rushed over and gave her a hug, "I couldn't have done it without you! But look at your gown! It's a mess!"

Serena gazed down at herself with a small gasp. "Oh well!" she said, swallowing hard. "Who cares about a silly old dress? Besides, I had so much fun!"

As Serena and Toby looked at the cakes together, Serena said wistfully, "You know, I've never been to a wedding."

"Come tomorrow!" Toby said.

"I will." Serena's eyes lit up. "You know something, Toby? You have a wonderful group of friends."

"That's for sure!" Toby agreed. "My Angel Club is the greatest!"

"So is mine!" Serena said, extending her wings. Then she flew up to the Exquisite and Heavenly Dress Shop to find something new to wear to the wedding.

14

A Horse-and-Tulip Wedding

The next day was sunny and warm, an absolutely perfect day for a wedding.

Mr. and Mrs. Antonio still felt a little wobbly, but they insisted on going. "I want to show off my daughter's cakes," bragged Toby's dad.

Toby put on her one fancy dress. It was green satin, and made a nice swishy sound when she walked. Her mom loaned her pearl earrings and a matching pearl necklace to wear with it. Rachel came over early and helped Toby do her hair.

"Your outfit is so pretty," Toby told Rachel, who was wearing a powder blue dress with a frilly white collar and cuffs.

They met Lulu and Val at the wedding.

"Lulu, you look like a candy cane!" Rachel teased. Lulu's dress was pink and white swirly stripes.

"And Val looks like a princess!" Toby declared. Val wore a long pink lace dress with a huge bow at the waist.

Toby looked around the church, wondering where Serena was.

"Here I am!" Serena said suddenly. She waved to Toby from the top of the organ pipes. Serena wore a dazzling violet gown with a long train that just missed tickling a man's bald head.

"Serena looks scrumptious!" Toby said to her friends as she waved to her guardian angel.

All through the ceremony, Serena cried into a lacy handkerchief. "Oh, it's so sweet," she kept repeating. "It's so sweet."

Toby noticed that Hortense didn't look nervous at all.

When Toby congratulated her and her groom, Hortense confided, "All during the ceremony, I pretended that Vic and I were on horseback. Lulu told me to try that, and it worked."

"Wait'll you see your cake!" Toby told her. "You'll love it!"

Toby was right. Hortense and Vic were ecstatic.

"Oh, those tulips!" Vic sighed romantically.

"Oh, those horses!" crooned Hortense.

Mrs. Heft told Mr. Antonio, "That cake is a work of genius."

"Well," he confessed, "the credit goes to my daughter, Toby."

"Thank you so much, Toby," Mrs. Heft said. "You are a multitalented young lady—a baker as well as a ballerina."

"How does she know that?" asked Toby, confused. She didn't remember Mrs. Heft ever asking about her ballet at the bakery.

"Oh," cried Mrs. Heft, a little flustered, "maybe I've said too much! Pay no attention to me. But I am looking forward to your dance recital next week. I love to see the arts flourish in Angel Corners. Thanks again for the cakes, Toby. They are adorable." And off she went to find the bride and groom for the cake-cutting ceremony.

All the guests were oohing and aahing around the tulip-decorated cake. Felicia's mother looked pale with jealousy as she congratulated Mrs. Heft on the beautiful little cakes.

"Angels' wings! How appropriate for an Angel Corners wedding," declared Mayor Witty.

"And it's not fattening—if you don't eat too much!" commented Derek Weatherby.

"I'm putting mine under my pillow," Lulu

announced. "There's an old custom that if you put a piece of wedding cake under your pillow, you will dream of your future husband."

"Yuck! What a mess!" Val said, making a face. "But maybe I'll do it, too. I hope I dream of Zeb!"

Toby's mother sat down with Toby's dad. She told him, "I've been thinking a lot about the bakery. Maybe we should start experimenting with a line of less fattening pastries, cakes, and cookies to lure back our customers. We could advertise them as 'Heavenly—and Healthy, too!'"

"Good idea!" agreed Mr. Antonio.

"Let's dance!" Rachel said, and grabbed Toby's hand. They went out onto the dance floor. Lulu and Val began dancing, too.

"Way to go, Angel Club!" Toby cheered, and they all high-fived right there on the dance floor.

CHAPTER

15

Feeling Like Heaven

Four days later, it was time for Toby's dance recital.

"Are you nervous?" Rachel asked her.

"Terribly," Toby said. "I feel like I have eight legs, and each one wants to dance in a different direction!"

"You'd better get over to the recital hall. I'll go pick up Andrea," Rachel said.

"I hope Val and Lulu remember to pick up Sylvie," Toby said.

"Of course they will! You just worry about your dancing!" Rachel grabbed Toby's hand. "You'll be great. See you backstage afterward."

Toby and Rachel went their separate ways.

Rachel reached Andrea's house in ten minutes. She knocked loudly at the door.

"Who is it?" a man with a deep voice answered.

"Um, it's Rachel. I'm a friend of Andrea's. I came to pick her up for the dance recital."

The door slowly opened. A tall, sandy-haired man stood there, looking perplexed. "I haven't heard anything about a recital," he said.

"I have!" said a dark-haired woman with glasses standing behind him. "Come in. I'm Andrea's mother. You must be Rachel Summers. Andrea's told me so much about you."

"I'll be right out," Andrea called from behind a closed door. The door opened and Andrea appeared, wearing a lovely pink skirt and a matching sweater.

"Where did you get that?" her father asked in a rough voice.

Andrea's mother answered for her, "From a good friend!"

"But I told you . . . we don't accept things from people. . . . If I can't buy them—"

"But, Dad," Andrea interrupted. "Everyone is going to be dressed up at the recital."

"That's right," her mother said, putting one of her arms around Andrea and the other around Andrea's father, "and these clothes were the wrong size for her friend. She wanted Andrea to have them so they wouldn't be wasted."

Andrea's dad gazed at Rachel, who was all dressed up, and then at his daughter.

The silence seemed to go on forever. Then he said softly, "Andrea, you look beautiful. And I see how badly you want to go. So how can I say no?"

"Oh, Daddy!" Andrea rushed over and hugged him. "I love you! I really do!"

"I know," he said with a small smile. "I love you, too. Go ahead, and have a good time."

"Come on!" Rachel grabbed Andrea's hand, and they rushed out the door together.

"Thank you for coming over!" Andrea said to Rachel.

They walked to the recital hall on Main Street.

As Rachel and Andrea entered the auditorium, Toby was already backstage.

Madame Maximova helped her into her dress, assuring Toby that it was okay to be nervous. "It gives you extra adrenaline for the performance. Besides, if you are not nervous, it means that maybe you do not care."

"Oh, I care!" said Toby, trembling. After she put on her makeup and did warm-up exercises, Toby looked out through one of the peepholes in the curtain. She could see the audience beginning to take their seats.

Toby found her parents and her brothers in the front row. Rachel and her mother were sitting in the second row with Andrea. The three seats next to Andrea were empty.

And now Val and Lulu were walking down the aisle with Sylvie, who was wearing a lemon yellow dress and party shoes.

Toby could see Sylvie give a little gasp when she noticed Andrea. Andrea's face lit up, but then she turned away.

Val, Lulu, and Sylvie filed into the row and sat down so that Sylvie was next to Andrea. Sylvie sat in her seat, staring straight ahead, but then she suddenly turned and faced Andrea with a smile on her face. Andrea reached out and grabbed Sylvie's hand and they both began talking a mile a minute.

"Yes!" Toby cheered. "Mission accomplished!"

Then she rushed back to finish her warm-ups. She felt a little less nervous, but her heart beat fast again when the music began.

"Serena, are you here?" Toby whispered.

"But of course!" Serena said. "I'll be up on the chandelier. It's the perfect view! Toby, you're going to dance divinely! I just know it."

When the curtain went up, the corps de ballet began dancing onto the stage. A burst of applause came from the front row where Mr. and Ms. McWithers sat. No one could miss Felicia McWithers. Somehow she had snuck onstage wearing her diamond earrings. They glinted in the lights, but they were instantly forgotten when Toby's music began playing, and Toby leaped onstage to begin her solo.

A ripple of pleasure ran through the audience at the sight of Toby and her feathery red and gold dress. But all Toby heard was the music. She danced as if she were a part of it.

She leaped and spun as well as she had when Serena had helped her in the attic. *But this time I'm doing it all myself!* Toby thought.

When her solo was finished, the whole auditorium burst into applause. The Angel Club stamped its feet in appreciation. Toby's mom and dad blew her zillions of kisses.

And up near the ceiling, Serena curtsied to Toby as if she were a queen.

Toby gracefully took her bows and curtsied back to Serena.

Madame Maximova presented Toby with a bouquet of roses.

Then suddenly a silver charm bracelet came flying down to the stage. It had one charm: a ballet dancer with silver angel's wings and high-top basketball shoes!

"Thank you, Serena," Toby whispered.

Then the curtain came down, and Toby's friends hurried backstage.

"Fine work!" said Madame Maximova. "I knew you wouldn't let me down."

"Fabulous!" Lulu, Val, and Rachel cried, hugging her over and over.

Sylvie and Andrea came over together. "Thank you," they both told Toby. "It was really sweet, what you did for us."

"You can thank the whole Angel Club," Toby said. "We did it together."

"Hey, Rachel, look!" Toby jingled her bracelet. "Serena gave me this."

"It's perfect!" Rachel said. "It's like my locket from Merrie." Her locket shone on the chain around her neck.

Val and Lulu watched them, both yearning for their angels to come.

"Don't worry!" Toby and Rachel said together, as if they could read their friends' minds. "Your angels are coming soon!"

"May I speak to you a moment?" Madame Maximova asked Toby. "Actually, Mrs. Heft wants to tell you something first."

"Yes, indeed." Mrs. Heft smiled. "Toby, first I want to tell you that I enjoyed the recital very much!

And just recently, a perfectly angelic thought came to me. Actually, I received a very thoughtful letter informing me that the arts in Angel Corners need some financial support, especially dance. So I've decided to endow Madame's ballet school with a dance scholarship."

"And," added Madame Maximova, turning to Toby, "I think that you are the perfect person to receive it."

"Really? Then I can continue my lessons?"

"That's right!" said Madame Maximova.

Mr. and Mrs. Antonio beamed. "You earned it, Toby! You worked so hard for it!"

"Yay!" All the members of the Angel Club cheered at Toby's good fortune. Serena applauded, too, though only Toby could hear her.

Toby glowed, feeling like she was floating miles above the ground.

After Toby changed out of Madame Maximova's costume, she and her friends went to the Antonios' house for a little party. Sylvie and Andrea sat together, chattering away. "Tomorrow, right after school, you're coming over to see my rabbit!" Andrea was telling Sylvie. "And I *mean* it this time!"

Toby told her friends in the Angel Club, "This has been such an amazing month!"

"Yes," Rachel said, "because your angel came!"

"But there were other angels, too," Toby said. "Earth angels. Lulu and Val were angels to write that letter to Mrs. Heft. You handed it to Hortense that day in the video store, right?"

"Right!" said Lulu and Val proudly.

"And," continued Toby, "that bakery salesman was an angel, too! If he hadn't left the heart-shaped pans here, I would never have gotten the idea for the little cakes."

"Right," said Val. "And don't forget Derek. He's the one who gave Lulu and me the idea to write that letter."

As all this angel talk was happening on earth, Serena was flying back up to the Angel Academy.

"Your first assignment was a great success!" Florinda said, greeting Serena with a huge hug.

"I had so much fun!" Serena confessed. "And it didn't matter that I wasn't perfect."

"That's right," Florinda told her. "You've learned a very great lesson! And now it's time for your special ceremony."

Florinda enfolded Serena within her wings and flew her to the Celestial Cafeteria.

"We are having a special banquet in your honor!" Florinda announced.

"Oh my!" Serena gasped at rows and rows of

tables covered with lacy pink cloths and heaps and heaps of red tulips! The angels all carried tulips as they filed in and sat down.

"It's so beautiful!" Serena crooned. "Will we have angel food cake for dessert?"

"Of course!" Florinda answered.

Then she presented Serena with a new pair of wings and a crystal locket with Toby's picture inside.

"Earth is wonderful!" Serena said. "There's no other place like it."

"I agree!" Merrie's eyes sparkled as she gazed at her locket with Rachel's picture inside.

"I hope it's my turn to go to earth soon!" said Amber.

"Me too!" chimed in Celeste.

"You will both be going very soon," Florinda assured them. "You have my word on that!"

The banquet went on long into the night, but Amber and Celeste spent much of their time gazing down at Angel Corners.

"Soon," they both said dreamily, "soon!"

Fran Manushkin is the author of more than thirty children's books. A native of Chicago, and formerly a teacher and children's book editor, she now lives in New York City with her cats, Niblet and Michael Jordan.

Angels really do exist!

Watch for book #3 in the
***Angel Corners* series**

Lulu's
Mixed-Up Movie

Lulu attempts to frame her father's girlfriend on candid camera, but life on earth—as in heaven—is not always as it seems in the movies.

Watch for book #4 in the
Angel Corners series

Val McCall,
Ace Reporter?

How could Val have written the nasty things she did in her debut newspaper column, jeopardizing even the loyalty of the Angel Club?